"This is a lovely story full of nice viv
well developed style and everything
scene setting/world building is good - make that great - rich and evocative,
dropping me right into the world. Quite a feat for an indie author ... "

-Lindsey Williams, *Motherhood*

"...Ash herself is a tough and resourceful character with a mysterious past. It left me wanting to read more!"

-Katherine Bryant, *Branna's Song: The Coldwood Saga*

"I find Ash to be an interesting character. She presents as a tough and savvy zombie hunter as she goes in search of stuff. In this book, what that constitutes the stuff is not revealed in its entirety. It is known that some of the stuff has to do with Ash's past. However, there are hints that Ash has another side to her."

-Stacy Overby, *Ambrosia: A Poetry Anthology*

Rising Ash

R.G. Westerman

ISBN-13: 978-0998185026

For

Sara and Kaif

You know why.

One

Tension burns in my arm as I take aim, lowering my gaze into the scope. I have been waiting in this tree for about an hour and finally something edible crosses my sights. Across from me on the far tree branch, the squirrel pauses, twitching its tail as if to taunt me. I take a slow breath, careful to keep my balance.

Seconds pass and the arrow flies from the crossbow hitting the mark, sending the creature tumbling into the underbrush. Small black birds erupt in a flurry from the brambles. I sit up straddling the branch and adjust the bow around to my back before I swing down, my feet finding the rocky ground.

The grass-grown gravel road curves through the field up ahead, dotted with a smattering of wet red leaves. I take a few labored steps towards the shadowed brick shelter up ahead, my legs sore from sitting in the tree for so long. Ivy and vines drape the trees in a chaotic tangle, grown over and filling the air with the scent of rotting wood.

I estimate there to be only a few hours of sunlight left. There is not much to accomplish for the day except to prepare and eat the parcel which I have just won. The meat will go a small way towards filling my stomach, but it is better than nothing. At least, the shelter up ahead would make a good place to settle in for the night. Careful of my steps, I skirt around the edges of the swamp, doing my best to stay undercover.

I have not seen a zombie in several hours. Even in my mind, I feel silly calling them that. The word sounds like something out of a story told long ago, a fairy tale from childhood, but these things, these creatures, living while yet dead and rotting, are all too real. I saw one a few miles back, crouching over the carcass of the yearling deer at the side of the road. That was a real shame. There would have been a lot of good meat on that deer.

I break through the underbrush, grab the arrow containing my night's meal and head towards the shelter. Having a means of hunting in which I could retrieve my ammo made life a great deal simpler in this world. Bullets, with their awkward explosive noise, always drew unwanted attention.

The storm clouds threaten to take over the sky, and fat rain drops splatter against the ground. I pick up my pace, quickly ducking into the wooden door of my shelter. Once inside I can relax my senses, something I still find difficult even after all these years. I do not expect to see any more of them for a while, as they tend to disappear when it rains. I leave the wooden door open, glad that I already have wood for a fire gathered on the dirt floor, at least enough to warm the small space and cook my food.

I nudge one of the branches with the black leather toe of my boot, before crouching to start the fire. Before long, I have the squirrel stripped and roasting on the spit leaning into the flickering yellow flames. I glance around, taking another quick assessment of the surroundings.

The shelter perches at the end of a row of brick houses alongside the back yard area of a much larger house, which possesses white columns and tall glass windows. I settle in at the doorway watching the storm clouds roll by overhead. Better to wait it out than to get caught in the rain closer into the city where shelter would be hard to come by. Here I can remain clear of any intrusions.

The scent of roasted meat fills the small space and my mouth waters in response. I tend to the fire and turn the makeshift spit, glad of the small amount of warmth generating from the source. I still have a small pouch of beef jerky left over from the last supply run, but that is the last of it. The yellow flames illuminate the space enough to cast shadows of the small cot and table lining the walls. Despite the presence of a wooden chair, I remain sitting on the floor, turning to face out and watch the falling rain darkening the patch of green grass outside my small hovel. I cannot see much beyond the hulking house ahead of me, but I know I have a secure vantage point in case anything approaches.

The fire sputters and a flame flares up as grease drops into the coals. Exhaustion creeps up on me, my shoulders and legs aching from the day's activities. I pull off my boots, followed by the damp socks, laying them out to dry and stretching my bare toes towards the meager warmth of the flame.

I decide the squirrel has cooked long enough and I pull it from the heat. My fingers singe as I attempt to pluck off pieces of the dark meat, but my stomach wins out. I know I need to replenish my supplies, but being this close to the city it will not be difficult to complete a supply raid in the next few days.

Carefully cleaning each bone and examining the carcass to make sure I don't miss a single morsel, my stomach calms its rumbling protest, satiated at last. I reach over and pull the heavy door closed as the darkness sets in. This will give me some amount of security during the night. Nothing can get in. That much is certain. Regardless, I pull the cot over in front of the door, tossing a handful of dirt over the dying fire. Instead of the cot, I opt to curl up on the dirt floor on the far side of the fire, falling asleep to the constant rain tapping against the wooden rooftop outside.

I wake to the sound of scratching around the door. The thin tendrils of dawn reach underneath the strip between the door and the damp floor. I immediately reach for my crossbow as I roll onto my feet. The instant adrenaline rush pushes me into full wakefulness, and I realize the sound, the slow scritching of mindless movements, is coming from a zombie outside.

For the moment I am safe, locked inside this shelter, so I take a moment to pull on my boots and locate my knives. The barricade of the cot against the door stayed in place through the night, but the creature beyond the door is blocking my primary means of escape. I move over to the window. It is long since painted shut, but I try it regardless.

Stuck fast.

From this vantage point, I do have a clear view of the front of the mansion, the large staircase leading up to the wide concrete porch framed by the tall white columns. I press as far to the right as I can, trying to gain a clearer view. My small movements are met with an increase in motion from the creature outside.

At the top of the staircase, I catch sight of a woman crouching with her back pressed up against the stately doorway of the mansion. A young boy clings to her. Even through the small distance between us, I can see the terrified look in both of their faces. They stay frozen in place, their faces caught in grimaces of terror. The woman has her arms wrapped around his shoulder, holding his head against her chest. His glassy eyes gaze wildly towards the front door of my small shelter. She glances towards me, her trembling eyes cutting towards my movement in the window. The boy keeps his gaze fixed on the thing in front of my shelter. For as far as I see, the grassy landscape around rolls into the distance without a sign of another one of them.

This one is alone. For now.

I have no way to get a viable shot on it. I cannot see it from the window. With some resignation, I know what I have to do. There is no other way. I place the crossbow on the bed and reach down to the knives inside my boots. With a blade in each hand, I move to the center of the room, pausing to listen. It shuffles back and forth, scraping its rotted, tattered shoes along the concrete floor. At least, it is staying away from the boy and the woman.

Okay.

I take a deep breath.

First, I slowly pull back the cot, scooting it out of the way with a loud scrape against the concrete. My fingers fumble with the small latch at the door. The ancient property has not been lived in for ages. I can only hope the door swings open in one motion. With one last breath, I tighten my grip around the handle of my knife and pull the door open.

Jumping back, I give myself enough space while the creature advances on me. In this small room, the sickly sweet stench of rotting flesh is nearly overpowering. It comes at me slowly and steadily; I circle around trying to keep the space between us. I have seen them often enough, the dead eyes, the rotting skin. This one has a flap of pink flesh hanging from its face and exposing the bone white jaws, teeth jutting from black ichor. The creature emits a small growl, nothing more than a gurgle deep in the back of its throat.

I leap forward and swipe at the creature's face, looking to gain purchase with my blade. I miss and it lunges towards me, teeth clamping dangerously close to my forearm. In my periphery I see the woman, staring at me with increased horror, clutching more fiercely to the boy. Her mouth forms a small circle, drawn tight against her teeth.

She nears panic.

If they make a sound and draw his attention, there is no guarantee that I can take him down before he gets to them. I need to dispatch this thing quickly. Hopefully, the small space can work in my favor. I lunge again swinging my knife with careful aim.

Right through the eyeball.

The knife lands without much fanfare, just a small squishy sound. When I pull the knife out the creature collapses at my feet, no longer a danger to me or anyone else in this world. I grab the crossbow, slinging it over my shoulder on my way out the door.

I see the woman's face collapse in relief. The threat is gone.

For now.

I leave the creature, stepping over it carefully. Once outside, I wipe the knife blade against the ground to remove the viscera before placing it back in the sheath.

"You two okay?" I call over to them.

She does not answer right away but gives a short quick nod.

"It's alright," I say as I walk over towards them, careful to keep my shoulders relaxed. Just because I removed the danger does not mean they see me as an ally. I learned a long time ago that approaching new people always poses a risk. The irony remains, even though every stranger could be a threat, it is safer to run with a group than alone. I pause at the bottom of the stairs, hands up in front of me with my palms out.

The woman stands and pulls the boy to his feet. He looks like he might be about seven years old. They are both frightfully thin. I smile when I catch his eye, raising my hand in a small wave.

"Where are the two of you headed?" I ask.

She does not answer right away. They both stand there watching me with obvious suspicion. I need to get her talking.

"I'm going into town myself," I continue. "Heading in on a supply run."

I reach behind me to my backpack and pull out the last scrap of jerky, literally the last piece. As if approaching a wild animal, I hold the food out to the little boy as I step up onto the first step. He eyes the food with rapt focus but glances up at her. She gives a slight nod, barely visible before he quickly snatches it from my outstretched hand.

"What's your name?" I ask, keeping my eyes on him.

He does not speak. She does. "My name is Rachel," she says. "This is Marcus."

"Ash," I reply. "We need to take shelter quickly. Where there is one like that it usually means more are coming. We need to get under cover and move on after they pass us by."

I did not want to say so, but as soon as the loner went down I sensed the shift in the air. A horde approaches. A big one, within a few miles at most. Rachel nods, clutching the boy close to her.

"We've seen them before," she says. "We're traveling East towards the ocean. There were five of us, but the car got overrun a few miles back. Marcus and I are the only ones who got out."

"I'm sorry," I say quietly.

She nods, but her stiff expression shuts down any more discussion of it.

"The ocean," I continue. "What's there?"

"Don't know. Some say it's safe there. Clean of any infection."

I turn and scan my eyes over the horizon. The highway cuts through the rolling hillsides. They will be here soon. We need to move quickly.

She turns to me, looking me over in a quick examination. I keep my eyes away, glancing to the ground in hopes that she cannot read my expression.

"How old are you, Ash?" she asks. "If you don't mind me asking. You can't be much older than..."

"Fifteen," I say hitching the straps of my crossbow around my torso. "According to last count, I'm fifteen."

I turn away from her shocked expression, facing towards the hilly valley just past the freeway. The shift in the air is so subtle that I cannot even pinpoint the movement in the trees or the distant sound that I know only I can hear. I gesture for the two of them to remain silent. Beyond the sound of the birds and the rustling of leaves, I hear them.

"We don't have much time," I say.

"What's happening?" Rachel asks as the boy continues to pull bites off his morsel of jerky.

I turn back and press against the door to the large mansion. Not much longer and this building will be surrounded by shuffling, broken-soled shoes, scuffling forward, mindless to whatever is in front of them, capable of no reason at all.

"We can't get in there," she says.

"Why not?" I ask.

"It's a historical building. The door is locked." She points to the large metal green sign which apparently explains the significance of the property. I had not taken the time to read it.

I pull my sleeve down over my hand, forming a fist which I use to punch through the window pane nearest the knob and unhook the lock. She winces at my actions, but seconds later the door swings open with ease.

"But..." she stammers.

"Everything is a historical building at this point," I say as I push open the door. "There's a horde over the horizon. I understand the sentiment. Really I do, we don't have time to find another place right now. They'll be here within the hour."

Her eyes dart wildly from me to the close horizon past the road. I see in her gaze that she expects any second for the creatures to appear, swarming over the hillside like a colony of ants. She nods and ushers the boy towards the open doorway.

Once inside, I find the largest piece of furniture, the ornate footed sofa, and scoot it in front of the door. I steal a glance towards the boy. The way he clings to her and watches me with those wide trembling eyes leaves me feeling unnerved. I move silently around the room double-checking the security of the windows. I wonder what they had been through. Obviously something, based on the pallid circles under his eyes.

"This room is secure," I say as I turn towards them. "Unfortunately, we are just going to have to wait them out as they pass by. The two of you should stay in the middle. I'll stay on watch just in case."

"Just in case of what?" the woman asks.

I glance down at the boy, nothing more than a flick of the eye. She nods, her expression drawn.

"Should we stay quiet?" she asks.

"It wouldn't hurt. I still haven't figured out what attracts them. I know they are not very smart. We can't be too careful, but I don't see them getting past the stairs."

The crash of breaking tree branches echoes from the hillside outside, propelling us all into motion. I cross the room and check the windows. The two of them lower slowly to the floor, landing in a cross-legged pile, arms grasping at each other. The fear in their eyes, downright palpable. I reach down to my belt and pull out the sheathed knife. I place my other hand around the crossbow and pull it around to my shoulder, wincing at the loud click when I remove the safety.

I see the first one appear over the horizon.

The horde moves at a snail's pace, lurching forward one step at a time. The front lines of them scatter here and there in chaotic wandering, but for the most part, they look like a sea, one entity mindlessly absorbing anything that crosses its path. The first of the pack reach the freeway two miles out and make their way across, one step at a time. One of them stumbles, and just like that, it becomes absorbed, trampled over by the others, no longer visible.

We could be here for a while.

The edges of the horde stretched to the horizon on either side, partially because of the narrow window impeding my vision. It is not very deep, maybe half a mile at most. I hold my breath as they near, keeping my eyes on the bottom of the stairs leading up to the front door where I stand, my crossbow at the ready, with nothing but the thin membrane of wood between me and them.

I have seen them take stairs before, but it involved several of them falling and forming a gruesome ramp. The others then gained traction eventually and made their way up that way. It could also mean they contained the capacity of brain function for problem-solving on some level. Either that or it was a fluke. Hopefully, it is the latter.

By this time the sound has reached all of our ears, the slow moan and shuffle, the grating pull of flesh against earth. The worst part is the mindlessness of their movements. I turn my eyes to the first step down below me as they shuffle forward.

The first wave makes it to the stairs.

Toes bump against the rise of the step. One falls forward and my breath catches in my throat. It makes no move to correct itself. The rest of them shuffle around it, moving towards the edge of the large house like water in a rocky stream bed. I exhale.

We all wait, none of us moving a muscle.

The view through the window is nothing more than sky and the endless sea of bobbing rotting heads; vacant eyes. The unnatural silence is broken only by the sound of their bodies, the machinations of animated flesh moving even in the midst of decay.

Bone scraping against bone for miles all around us.

Marcus takes a breath, nothing more than a hitch. Rachel clutches his shoulders. I turn and catch his eye, silent.

Don't move. Don't make a sound. I will the thoughts towards him, hoping that my expression is enough for him to read. He nods, just once. I turn back to the window.

After several minutes the horde begins to dissipate, winding to just a few stragglers. Finally, the last one disappears out of range.

"I think they are gone," I whisper. They both let out audible breaths. It would be another hour before it would be safe to leave the mansion. I turn away from the window and sit down with them.

Two

"Were the two of you headed into town also?" I ask as I turn back towards the window. The sky had become a dull slate blue, but clear as far as I could see, excellent weather for a supply run.

"Yes," she begins. "I'm afraid we lost our food with the car also. We had been on the open road for a couple of hours before you found us. I didn't think we would have survived for very much longer if you had not shown up when you did."

"I didn't do much of anything," I say as I stand, brushing the dust off my jeans. "I just happened to be in the right place at the right time."

"Would you come with us?" Rachel asks. "Safety in numbers, and all that?"

I glance at the two of them, taking stock. Survival depends on having a group, even a small one can make all the difference. I see no visible weapons between them, nothing showing any particular speed or skills in a fight situation. I already know they would slow me down to some degree. If we did join up, it would be to their benefit. I would have to be careful.

Marcus' eyes dart around the room, his shoulders momentarily relaxed now that the excitement had passed. Rachel is right. They would not have survived much longer.

"Okay, sure," I say. "I think we can watch out for each other."

They both nod.

"First thing's first. We need to find a vehicle. Yours is out of commission?"

"We lost it a few miles back to the West."

"Do you have any belongings there? Anything you need to go back for?"

"No." A flicker of emotion passes over her face, but just as suddenly it is gone.

"Just as well," I say. "I want us to keep moving. I was in the process of circling the outskirts of town, but after that horde, I think we should follow the path they took."

"Do you think that's safe?" she asks. "What if one of them circles back?"

"They don't travel that way. When there are that many together, they keep moving forward. They go over or around anything that blocks their way. But never back. If they do veer away, it's off to the side. I've learned it is safer to follow a horde as long as we keep our distance. They actually did us a favor."

"I don't know, I still think the road would be a better option," Rachel says.

"This way is clear. We can't know the same about the road."

"I see." She swallows hard, making a thick clicking sound in the back of her throat before she nods.

"Marcus," I say, as I crouch down to his eye level. "I'm going to need some help from you."

"Me?" he replies, scrunching his nose up at me. This is the first time I have heard him speak.

"Yes, you. Can you tell me, what is your favorite color?"

"Um..." He scrunches up his nose as if considering the

importance of the question. "Blue?"

"Are you asking me or telling me?" I add a small grin in an attempt to ease his discomfort.

"Um... I'm telling you." He stands a bit straighter, firming up his shoulders. "I like blue."

"Okay great, Marcus. You know what we are going to do once we get into town?"

"What?"

"We have to find a car. There's going to be a whole lot of cars and other vehicles there. All different colors. What about we keep an eye out for the shiniest blue car we can find. Sound like a plan?"

He nods vigorously with a grin on his face.

"Okay," I whisper. "It's go time."

We step out the front door. I keep the crossbow at my side in case we run into any trouble. After scanning the horizon and taking account of the small breeze, I motion for them to follow. I stay in front, tracking the path after we leave the mansion. Marcus walks behind me with Rachel bringing up the rear. I reach into my back pocket and give her my other switchblade, but this is mostly a gesture on my part. I do not have much faith in her abilities as a fighter, even if she does put in a good effort. The sun is bright. Now and then a bird chirps, alerting me that we are traveling in the right direction. The time to worry is when the birds go silent.

"Have you eaten?" I ask.

"Not since the car broke down. About an hour before maybe. We had found our way into an abandoned grocery store."

"That's good. We'll keep an eye out for something quick for

you guys."

The next place we come to is an old diner, surrounded by trees and vines already making their way toward pulling the walls down, snaking through the windows like bony fingers. Eventually, the whole world will look like this. That is what I have learned by growing up in a dead world.

Nothing lasts.

Everything falls.

Everything.

The boy, Marcus, must have been born around the same time that everything went to hell. A child of the Fall. They are rare, as there are not many of us left, but there is something remarkable about the children who have only known this world, some kind of steeliness, absent in those who remember.

"Where did you come from, Rachel?" I ask. "Before, I mean. Before...you know."

"Cincinnati," she answers. "I was in insurance sales."

"Insurance sales?"

"It's not even worth explaining," she says with a small laugh.

A shuffling of branches catches my attention off to the left. The others freeze instantly and I reach for my bow swinging it around into position like I have done a thousand times. The trees surrounding us block out the view. We stand in the center of a small grove, grown up with briars, flattened a bit by the passing horde, but tangled and thick regardless.

Marcus backs into Rachel, and I see her fingers tighten around the handle of the knife tucked into her belt, clutching his shoulder with her other hand. Her eyes dart from me to the origin of the sound.

A mare steps into view, lining up perfectly with the cross hairs of the eyepiece. A sense of relief washes over me, but I cannot relax yet.

I take aim.

Seconds later, the leaves behind her come alive as her tiny foal trots out next to her. I exhale and lower my bow casting a glance towards the other two. We could use the food, of course, but seeing the wonder light up on Marcus's face at the sight of the baby horse let me know I made the right decision in sparing them. If either of the animals had been injured, or if the foal had been alone, things would have been different. This time, I would pass. We watch them in silence until they canter off into the surrounding thicket.

A short time later, we arrive at a small, square building. The first thing I notice is the open door, always a sign of danger.

"Wait here," I say. "It could be infected. I'll need to clear the building to be sure."

"Are you sure?" Rachel asks. "You can't go in there alone. At least, let me follow you."

That is the last thing I want. "I've done this many times. It will only take a few minutes. Keep your back to the wall and stay here until I get back."

Her eyes dart around the surrounding landscape before finally landing back on me.

I nod, hoping to give her a sense of ease. I pulled the knife from my ankle strap and stepped into the darkened shadows.

I hear no sounds except myself pounding on the walls and scraping my knife blade along the walls in an attempt to draw them out if there are any. I make my way through the main room with the blade held up ready to strike when necessary as I push open the swinging doors to the kitchen. With the amount of dissonant noise I have made, they would have shown themselves by now.

Finally, I stand in the center of the room satisfied that the property is secure.

"Come on in," I call, sticking my head out to the two of them standing side by side against the wall of the building. "It's clear."

I lock the door behind me, noticing both of their faces relax at the relief of not having to be on guard for a few moments. Marcus navigates over to one of the padded plastic booth seats and sits down, taking off his shoes and rubbing his feet.

Rachel walks with me as I began to double check the perimeter. Now that the place was secure of anyone, or anything, besides us, we need to make sure no one could get in, either. We check the windows, one at a time, running our hands along the panes of glass, testing the edges. Nothing appears broken or loose so far.

We come to the swinging doors leading into the kitchen. Before we push through, she glances back at the boy who stares open-mouthed at the bright logo hanging above the long dead video game.

"He'll be fine," I say.

She nods as we push into the darkened kitchen.

Our only hope was to find something canned. If the old stoves had worked, this place would have been an ideal place to set up camp. It may yet be, even without the power. I step forward and start opening doors, pulling out bowls and any kitchen tools I find.

The gadgets look foreign and awkward in my hands, and I can only guess what their purpose might be. The first thing that comes to mind is how I could use each one as a weapon. At the end of the cabinets, I see an open door leading into a pantry area.

"Rachel," I say just loud enough to catch her attention across the large kitchen. She steps over and her mouth drops open at the sight before us.

The small room is full of shelves, stocked full of food. A variety of soups, dry potato flakes, a collection of salad dressings, cornmeal, beans, canned chicken, fish and more. The amount of food is enough to feed us for a good long while.

"Too bad none of it is fresh," Rachel says in jest, her voice tinged with wonder.

"I have an idea," I say. "I know the two of you are heading east, but what if we stayed here for a few days?"

"Stayed here? What do you mean?"

"I mean, I know it isn't wise to stay in one place for too long, but this food is just sitting here. We can easily secure the building. It wouldn't take much more. All we would need is just a source of heat. Marcus has already discovered the booths are more comfortable than the bare ground. Maybe even just until we get our strength back. What do you think? We work on this stash here until it is manageable for us to carry the rest."

"Hmm." She considers the idea for a moment. "We have

been on the road for a while now..."

"Just a few days time," I say. "Then we will move on once we feel rested."

"Okay, yeah. I think it would be good for him. He's been through more than enough. It's a great idea, the more I think about it. When are we ever going to see this much food in one place again?"

We start to pull things down from the shelves. Just a few cans at first. I reach for a cardboard box of apple juice and cradle it in my left arm, piling smaller cans on top of it.

"Marcus," she calls through the door, keeping her voice muted.

He appears a moment later with curiosity etched on his face. Seeing the stash, his eyes grow wide and his mouth falls open.

"Come here," I say as I beckon him to the kitchen.

I take the juice to the main counter, grabbing a knife on the way. After I slice open the top of the box, I reach over to the dish area and grab a glass. He watches as I pour the amber liquid into the glass and hand it to him.

He drinks it with a kind of enthusiasm that I have not seen in awhile from anyone. He empties the glass, leaving a few droplets on his lips, which he wipes away with the back of his hand. I fill it again and he repeats the whole process happily.

The reasons I have given Rachel about staying here are only partially true. I want to make the run into town without them, and keeping them in a secure location would make that easier.

I do not believe they would hinder me. I need to find us a

car, of course, but I needed something else as well. I had to find what I was looking for, and that, I have to do alone. It gave me some small inkling of peace that the child would not be out in the open. This was no world for a child. I would do what I could to get them a secure vehicle and get them headed on their way.

When humanity disappeared, they left behind all of their belongings for us survivors to pilfer. Of course, this abundance of stuff does not always guarantee survival. Though we have plenty of things surrounding us--cars, houses, clothes, weapons--what we have a shortage of is food, the one thing we need the most. I already know the key to long-term survival is to find a way to live.

The problem is, our world is poisoned. Though we can get by on a daily basis, the end game is already decided. We may survive today, but what of tomorrow? This infection scouring its way through humanity decided our fate from the beginning. I may survive, but I am only one. Eventually this poisonous world will take the last of us.

Rachel had asked me how I knew about the creatures, about their behavior. Truth is, I have no idea how I know. Everything has always just been there, an instinct which I have never understood. My childhood was nothing more than fragmented bits and pieces, flashes of memory that held little to no meaning for me.

The taste of hot oatmeal.

A smiling woman holding my hand in a moving elevator.

The flash of the sun reflecting off a moving vehicle.

I know something is there. I just need to find a way to unlock it.

"There is still plenty of daylight left," I say. "I'm going to go out and collect some wood. I think we can build a small fire pit in one of the stoves for cooking."

"Yeah," she replies. "I'll take stock of the food. I'm sure I can make something out of the ingredients here. Once upon a time, I was quite talented in the kitchen."

"He could probably use some rest." I nudge my head towards Marcus, merrily pouring himself another glass of apple juice.

"Perhaps you're right." She considers the boy, turning back to me with a look of concern on her face. "A fire. Inside?"

"This place is made from tile and metal. As long as we keep a barrier around it, we'll be fine. We can all use a hot meal. I think we are good for today, but tomorrow I'll go out and find us some fresh meat."

"That sounds good." She stretches her arms overhead, stifling a yawn. "I can't remember the last time we were in a safe place like this. Not having to keep watch for a cluster or a horde. Not to mention having an actual kitchen. You may be the crack shot hunter, but when it comes to the kitchen, this is my domain. You worry about getting us a heat source and I'll put together some food for all of us."

"Okay then." I cannot help but smile at her enthusiasm.

I step back out to the restaurant area. The windows still have glass in them, which is rare. Buildings either have them broken out or have vines taking over. Most places along the edge of town are already starting to grow over.

I have heard rumors of places that had more security, walls around towns, protected communities, larger groups of people taking care of each other. Until such time as I can find such a place, I have to take extra steps to secure my location down to one entrance. If the creatures do breach the security, it forces them into a bottleneck. I can manage them that way.

I find the long bench and pull it with some effort to the side door. The glass walls of the restaurant are not a secure perimeter, but I know if I can patch it up a little we can use the kitchen as our main hideout. Also, despite its fragility I have never seen one of them walk through a pane of glass, as of yet.

I step back into the kitchen where Marcus and Rachel are collecting ingredients and taking inventory of the supplies.

"I've got this area secure for now," I say. "I'm going out for firewood."

Rachel raises her eyebrow. "Will you be okay?" she asks.

"Oh, yes. I've done it many times. I can handle it."

"Okay," she replies.

I find it remarkable that we have developed such as easy camaraderie in such a short time. Then again we have known each other for nearly a day already. For some, that is already a lifetime in this world.

Carefully, I exit the front door, making sure the landscape is clear before moving forward. I spy the old iron bench tipped over on its side, which I pull in front of the doorway behind me as a makeshift blockade. It is large enough to fit over the edges of the two front doors, enough to keep the creatures out. Rachel and Marcus can still escape if need be. I dust the remnants of rust off my palms as I glance over the setup. I feel pretty good about the security. I still have my crossbow and my knife. Rachel still has the other knife if they should need it.

Collecting wood does not take long at all, and I return with an armload. I step gingerly back over the bench to get back inside. We have to build the fire inside the stove in order to cook the food, but the metal walls would keep it contained, easily managed.

I arrive in the kitchen to find Rachel has produced a collection of wraps, waiting to be roasted once we got the fire going. She and Marcus stand over the counter covering each in foil to tuck them into the coals for roasting.

Marcus helps build the base, carefully placing the small branches underneath the larger logs. I produce a lighter out of my pocket. I always carry several as these are one of the items incredibly easy to find. Within minutes, the fire blazes inside the confines of the large, industrial sized oven.

Rachel uses a pair of large tongs to place the wraps into the heat. They turn out pretty good, although we have to be careful not to burn our fingertips when opening them. She had managed to find, among the stash, some cans of refried beans, tomato sauce and a collection of starchy vegetables, corn, mashed potato flakes, mixed and wrapped into soft tortillas. It makes for a filling, high protein meal.

"These taste good," I say between mouthfuls.

"Don't sound so surprised," she replies.

Marcus peels away the aluminum before each enthusiastic bite. I watch him, wondering when he last had a hot meal. We eat in silence. I can see their faces becoming more relaxed with the knowledge of our safety, even if it is temporary.

Three

Marcus picks the lower level of the stainless steel rolling table as the place he wants to sleep. I place the leftover's in the corner before I head back to the main part of the restaurant to finish securing the perimeter while Rachel tucks Marcus in. In the looming silence of the oncoming night, I hear her sing to him. She has found a pile of clean aprons and tablecloths to build a small nest for him. The fire, now nothing more than glowing embers, would be enough to keep us warm until morning.

Rachel joins me after a few moments, pushing quietly through the swinging door from the kitchen.

"Need some help?" she asks.

"I'm nearly finished, I think."

All of the furniture is pushed against the windows, creating a semblance of a wall around us and removing the possibility of a breach.

"Looks good," she says glancing around the room.

The restaurant looks strangely bare. I sit down on the small staircase leading from the bar area down to the empty center. Rachel sits down next to me.

"How's Marcus doing?" I ask.

"He's sleeping now. I've never seen him go out so fast. We've had a hard road lately. I'm glad he is safe for tonight."

"That's good."

"How long have you been out there?" she asks.

"I don't know. A long time I think." I glance over. She is watching me with intensity behind her expression, lips pursed, eyebrows drawn together. “I, um... I can't remember a lot of things.” I tap on the side of my head with my fingertip. “It comes and goes.”

“What happened?” she asks. “I mean before. What was your life like? How did you end up alone?”

“That's one of the things gone. I have a few flashes, but that's about it.”

“You must have some idea.”

“Not really. I mean, I remember a woman wearing white. I can't remember her face, just kind of a presence. That's about all. I remember being younger, much younger, and she read to me and I felt safe. That's all I know.”

“Was she your mother?”

“I don't think she was.”

“You have been out in this from the beginning?”

“I suppose I have.”

Rachel shifts, adjusting to face me. “Let me ask you a question. Earlier, you said you would go out and collect firewood.”

“Right.” I feel a nudge of suspicion.

“I asked if I could help and you said no. I know it is dangerous out there, but even so, why didn't you let me come with you? It's safer if we all stay together.”

I turn away from her, staring forward. “I understand what you are thinking. To you, I look like a young girl. I get it. But I've been out there. You have seen that I can handle myself.” I trust her to an extent, but I don’t want to tell her everything. Not yet.

“It felt strange, I'll admit. Watching you leave. Not knowing if you would come back.”

"Let's say you came with me," I reply. "Let's say you and Marcus came along. Then we get caught somewhere. Who would you choose?"

"What do you mean, who would I choose?"

"I'm just a child," I say. " I know that. I'm a fighter and so far, a survivor, but I'm still just a girl. You feel on some level as if I need protecting. I know what I look like, skinny and small. I know how I come across to others. A little girl in need of protection, right? Would you say that was your first impression?"

"Alright. Yes, a little bit. Yes."

"But, despite all of that, if it comes down to it, and one of us is in danger. Who would you choose?"

The dawning appears on her face, eyebrows raising slightly.

"It's okay though. I do better when I'm alone actually."

I stand and cross the room, gazing through the windows shading my eyes against the glare of the glass.

"Tomorrow I'll go and find us a car," I say turning back to her. "You are okay with the arrangement for now?"

"Are you kidding me?" she says crossing her arms over her knees. "Ash, you're the best chance we've got."

"What do you mean?"

"We got hit hard before you found us. I mean, we lost our car, but the worst part was losing our group. We barely made it to that mansion. We just made it up the stairs, trying to find a place to rest, when that loner showed up. If you hadn't been there, we would have been caught in that herd. Now here we are, and within the day, we have found a secure building full of food. If it weren't for you, we'd probably be dead. No joke."

I nod, a bit taken aback by her sudden declaration of confidence. "Okay, fair enough. I'm glad for that, too."

She responds with a small smile.

"I'm going to get some sleep," I say. "It's been a bit of a big day, and tomorrow won't be much different if I'm heading into town."

"Okay then," she replies. "I'm going to stay up for a bit."

I slip into the kitchen where Marcus is snoring softly from his nest under the table. I think, I could have rolled the entire stainless steel contraption across the room and he would not have woken. I wander over to the fire, still putting out a good amount of heat. Then I find my way over to the pile of aprons and table cloths.

Part of me wants Rachel to come back into the kitchen so I could sleep in the outer room. I shuffle around for a few moments before I slip back to the door, peeking out at her. I watch her sitting on the stairs, leaning her chin on her hands. The weariness of her lot is etched on her face,. I know that feeling, that desire to give up. More often than not, it becomes overridden by the desire to survive.

The next morning, I climb off of the pallet where I had slept. I wake before the others, sliding the strap of my bow onto my back and slipping quickly out of the kitchen into the main room. Once again I find myself hoping they will stay put. They have nothing more to do today than to stay inside and remain alive. I set out a carton of powdered eggs, knowing Rachel would find the gallon jugs of water in the pantry. They might taste a little stale, but who would be picky at this stage of the game.

I am careful not to make a sound as I pull open the door to the outside, double-checking the placement of the iron bench. I step over it, pulling the door closed behind me before I turn to scan the horizon. Half a day has passed since the horde came through. Travelling down the road this time will be more beneficial instead of following the flattened ground, especially since I am now on the lookout for a car, a blue one if I keep my word to Marcus.

But a vehicle is not all I am looking for.

I jog across the parking lot pavement to the nearest road turning and keeping pace. My legs and lungs burn with the exertion as I near the middle of the city. It feels good. The fresh air helps clear my head as I make my way down the road, ever alert.

They could be anywhere.

Up ahead I see movement on the road.

At first, I think it is another deer or a badger or something. Not until I get close enough, do I realize that it is a zombie, crouched over a raccoon at the side of the road. Shame I had not gotten there first;I have never eaten raccoon before. I have my crossbow, but at this close range, I can save the arrow.

I pull out my knife as I slowly reach down and pick up a handful of pebbles. Hitching back my arm, I take aim and toss one of the small rocks over the monster's head so it lands on the other side of him. The sound catches its attention, and its head cranes up toward the noise.

I toss another handful of pebbles sending them skittering across the pavement. The creature stands and shuffles towards the sound. I take advantage of the distraction and stalk up behind it, taking slow, sideways steps. Then I spike the knife into the side of its head.

I feel vindicated each time I take one down. One less to worry about. Not that I had to worry about them, but I did not want Rachel or Marcus to know about that just yet. I stand up and walk forward toward the town. Up ahead, I can see the tops of the buildings rising beyond the horizon. Long lost skyscrapers, now just empty tombs jutting towards the sky.

The world as I know it has no more hope left within it. I often wonder what my life would have been like if the Fall of humanity had never happened. I collected bits and pieces over the years of what it might have been like. The lay of the cities alone gives me enough information. They were a busy lot, the people who lived before. The sheer number of vehicles left abandoned in their tracks gave evidence of rushing here and there.

A few years ago, I found some pictures from a school I had found inside one of the large buildings. The empty halls were lined with photographs of children, groups of about thirty, with one adult standing next to them, all of them smiling out at me. I can only guess what the purpose was of the pictures or what the role was of the adult. I remember trailing my fingers over the faces behind the smooth glass, wondering what their lives consisted of, what they talked about.

I remember little, but I still recall the presence of the woman in white. She showed me kindness, how to fight, and how to protect myself. These traits had always been something I assumed everyone had been taught, but as I move through this world, I learn over and over again that this is not the case.

The familiarity of my surroundings increases the closer I get to the middle of the city. The buildings loom around me now as I walk down the center of the street, subconsciously following the yellow, painted double line. Keeping the space around me, away from walls and windows, ensured that nothing would reach out and grab me. Here and there I see a few of them clustered and stranded under shadowed corners, unable to turn, reaching through bars of windows and vents, through the grating on the sidewalks and alongside the buildings.

I ignore them and move toward my destination. The roads, the signs, the shapes of the buildings, all become increasingly familiar as I walk. The building had once been a hotel, yet another piece of evidence that leads me to believe there had been more people to fill a building this size. The glass doors welcome me, as friendly as the maniacal grin of a carnival clown.

I push open the doors and step into the lobby.

The flash of returning memories nearly kicks me back off my feet. The glare of the sun on the marble floor. The new dusty smell of the chemicals permeating the building. I remember that the upper half of the building had been converted into apartments, where most of the doctors and scientists lived. It creeps up on me slowly, the realization that the entire structure had once been a self-sustaining community. Shops, grocery, and clothing on the first three floors. Then the laboratories on the floors above the arboretum. It all comes back, tumblers in a lock falling into place opening up the doorway to my memories.

My stomach drops with a feeling of vertigo as a memory of an elevator washes over me. I reach out and catch myself against the back of a faded chair. The table in the center of the lobby is rotted through; the legs lay crooked and broken, the top askew against the marble floor. I have a sudden vision of myself as a child, surrounded on all sides by mirrored glass, my own face, curving away into infinity. My hand is tucked into the hand of the woman in white standing next to me, warm and happy as she smiles down at me. She has a crinkle around her eyes. As clear as day, I see the curve of her lips, the whiteness of her teeth.

The elevator doors open and we step out, turning left. I see a flash of the office door within my hazy memory.

Room 642. That is where I need to get to. I shake my head and look up at the high vaulted ceiling above the now empty balconies. Darkened shadows seem to move in the tomb-like silence.

The elevators are out of service. Good thing I know where the stairs are. I cross the lobby to the small green door behind the elevators. I know better than to just open it outright. A building of this size and height would not be fully abandoned. Not completely.

Slowly I slip the handle of my knife into the palm of my hand before reaching for the door knob. The weight of the crossbow is comforting against my back. I know I won't be able to use it in the close quarters, but at least I know where it is. Part of me wishes I still had the other knife too, the one I had left behind with Rachel and Marcus. But they need it. I would find a way to make do. I open the door quickly with my weapon raised, prepared for the possibility of a mini-hoard pressing against it from the stairway.

It is vacant.

I exhale, taking careful steps forward, making my way onto the first landing. I turn and note the number on the door behind me. L1. A staircase leads up to the next landing while another leads down into the basements. I had never been down there, but I recall there are several levels of sub-basements.

I stop and listen.

If there is anything moving in the upper levels, I cannot hear it. The same cannot be said for the basement. The growling, grasping, sickeningly slick sounds of the creatures rises up from the lower levels. That many caught together, unable to escape, have most likely turned on each other. I can only imagine what horrors the lower levels have become. Nothing but a mass of rotted bones and decaying meat, writhing on itself in the ultimate orgy of the macabre.

I press myself against the wall, glancing upward, keeping my free hand on the strap of my crossbow. Close quarters often make for difficult self-defense. I stretch my neck around, trying to gauge the six flights I have to climb to get to my destination. Back to the wall, eyes upward, I move forward one careful step at a time, unable to fully see what may be around the corner. I make it to the second landing.

And then the third.

If it comes down to it, I know I can slip back into the doorway mirroring the one I had entered on Level One, although that would put me back into another place I would have to clear out. Might as well stay put, I decide. By the time I get to the fourth landing, I start to hear a distant rasping sound. Scratches against a concrete wall. Bloodied fingertips pressing against the surface, acting out the illusion of life itself. They just know forward; I think to myself. Nothing more. They have become so status quo, I hardly consider a solitary one to be much of a danger anymore. Regardless I do not like to be around them any more than I have to.

I ascend up to the next level. Up ahead, I can see it, trapped on the landing, walking back and forth adjacent to the door. Running into the corner wall, turning on shuffling feet and back towards the other wall. And again. Back and forth like a broken toy. I watch him for a few minutes, noticing it leaves a nasty red smudge of viscera behind every time it touches a part of the wall.

By the the level of decay, it has been trapped here for a while. I could not fathom how it became trapped in the first place, as there are no marks on the stairs either coming or going. It wears a standard lab coat, long since faded brown with blood and dirt. I would have to kill it if I wanted to get by, even though the thought of getting close to it makes my stomach do flip flops.

I wait until it turns away from me before I take the last few steps to the landing. Moving in quick strides, I pike it in the fleshy hollow between the ear and the jawline, wincing as the black ichor spurts out. It falls limp. I am able to pull my knife out before it wobbles and pitches over the side of the railing, spinning in a gruesome free fall to the lower levels. At any rate, that would give the others down there something new to munch on.

The last two flights have no noticeable threats. I make my way up to the level, still holding my knife, and keeping my eyes open. Another doorway marked L6 in those large blue letters. I stop at the door and place my ear as close as I can.

I hear nothing.

Except that the door is remarkably thick, enough to block out any noise perhaps. I test the door handle. Not locked. The security system shut itself off long ago. I open the door and step through. The vacant hallway stretches out on either side of me.

642.

If there are, in fact, forty-two rooms on this level then I have my work cut out for me. I try to stretch my mind to allow a flow of memories, which might make it easier for me to find my way around. I have been here before. That much is certain, but I have no recollection of how or when. Relying only on guesswork, I turn right, taking my time down the hallway. I do not hear anything threatening retreating or moving around, but I have been fooled before.

I always have my senses on high alert,. I cannot stay against the wall as I had in the stairway as there are doors on either side, some open, some closed, none of them locked. Papers and broken vials spill out into the hallway, an indication of the panic which set in when the world fell.

The hallway echoes silence as I move forward.

I cannot hear anything other than the sound of my own footsteps, scraping against the floor and displacing the papers and glass shards. They would have been one of the first to evacuate. I have a small flash of memory of this location in the hallway, something to do with the alarm. I can very nearly hear the sound of the dim buzz echoing off the walls.

Someone had grabbed my hand. I could not have been any older than seven or eight.

I recall pulling the pillowcase from the bottom of my bed

before I was whisked away. First the elevator. We were running, surrounded by the chaos of people all around us, all trying to escape, but with nowhere to go. Then a car. I was shoved forward into the back seat. I recognized the driver as one of the attendants from the laboratory.

Voices talking fast.

"Get her to safety. Follow the plan!"

"I'll meet you at the rendezvous."

"Go, just go!"

We drive fast, trees moving past the windows faster than I had ever seen. Had I been in a car before then? What had my life been like? I have no memories beyond that.

The sun streams through the wide glass window, locked forever now that the security system was shut down. Finally, I see the hallway where I would find the place I seek. Room 639 crosses my vision. Not far now. I keep walking down the hall, counting the doors until I see the number I need. 642.

The door stands ajar, and I push against it, keeping my ears alert to any sounds. I tap carefully on the wood, trying to revive anything that might be lurking within. At first, it looks just like any other office on the floor. I pull the door open as wide as it will go. Across the room, a large desk fills the other half.

That is her desk, I realize. The woman in white.

I walk forward, oddly mesmerized by the unexplained feeling of vertigo washing over me. The whole office looks like it had been turned upside down. Papers, the contents of her filing cabinet, strewn about, covering the floor. Beneath the papers, I see a flash of the red oriental carpet, which solidifies the idea that I have been here before.

On the surface of her desk, I see a framed photograph turned away from me, the only thing left standing. Her computer is overturned onto its side, the monitor screen staring up at me like a dead, gray eye.

I pick up the picture frame and turn it over, rubbing my hand across the glass, smearing the dusty surface. I see the face of the woman staring back at me with a smattering of freckles over her nose, blond hair coiffed into a low bun. Her teeth matches her white lab coat.

The woman's left hand was wrapped around the hand of a small child, a girl with her gap-toothed grin shone just as ferocious as the woman's. She had been laughing when the picture was snapped, taken just days before the Fall. I crack the glass against the edge of the desk, pulling the photograph out and quickly tucking it into my shirt before I scramble out of the room.

It does not take long for me to get out of the building, knowing the stairs are still clear. I have what I need, but I keep my knife out and ready as I make my way back down the stairs. I sprint across the lobby and push my way into the street, squinting against the brightness of the sun.

I remember that little girl in the picture. I remember the way she had laughed when the photographer held up the funny bird puppet. I know that she had laughed that day, for the last time in a long time. I know what happened that day because the picture was taken on the day the world changed. I had grown up in this building. My search for answers has only just begun.

Four

Standing in the middle of the road, the sun gleams off the dusty glass exterior of the tower and memories slowly start to come back. I face the building clutching my crossbow against my chest for comfort. My grip tightens on the handle of my bow. It all comes back, the memory of being here before, that same little girl clutching the hand of the woman in the white coat. Margaret Donovan.

I remember her. She is the woman who has appeared in my dreams, the vision in the elevator. Her office had been one of those rooms which felt like a shrine to the adult who inhabited it, silent and solemn. I brush my fingers over her face in the picture before I tuck it into the side pocket of my backpack.

I turn, walking at a slow pace down the center yellow line of the road, mulling the memories over. I used to live in that place. That woman, Margaret, had taken care of me, raised me I think. She was not my mother, though. I had a room, books, toys... this is where my childhood took place. This had been my home.

I make my way down the road eyeing the cars, parked on the side of the road, abandoned on the day humanity died. I see movements here and there in the shadows. The creatures, the zombies, tend to get stuck in the nooks and crannies, less of a threat than they would be out in the open.

Up ahead I spot a sky blue pickup truck veered off the road, nose first, into a small bridge over the ditch. There is no sign of impact. As I get close, I notice that the driver's side door hangs open and the poor creature is still buckled inside. Though the macabre scene is one of this undead man pulling against the seat belt, he must have been quite a character during his living days if the sideways jaunt of his cap of his hat means anything. His face appears skeletal covered with a thin layer of decayed gray flesh. A papery flap of torn cheek-flesh jiggles against his chin each time his body jolts forward.

I circle towards the creature inside the truck. On his dashboard sits a small plastic woman wearing a hula skirt and a tiny painted bikini top. Gold plastic stickers spell the name 'Buddy' across the front of the glove box. I spike my knife into his temple. His body goes limp, hanging against the taut seat belt.

"Sorry, Buddy," I say. "I need your truck."

My shoulder brushes against him as I reach across to unbuckle him. His head lolls from side to side as I maneuver his body out of the way. With his weight pulling against the strap, I have difficulty pushing the release button. Finally, it gives way and he falls forwards, lurching towards me. For a moment I think I missed his brain stem and perhaps he still has some semblance of movement in him yet. For a split second and I think I made a fatal mistake of being too casual about my kills. We tumble to the ground and I push him off to the side, lifeless and still, his mouth nothing but a bloody gash across his desiccated face.

The keys are still in the ignition, just where I had hoped they would be. The truck rumbles to life as the keys turn under my fingers, louder than I feel comfortable with. I know I need to get out of here before it draws attention from the roaming zombies. I get out onto the road, heading towards the nearest strip mall for supplies.

Now that I have a vehicle, it will take me only about ten minutes to get back to the others, so I still have plenty of time for a supply run before the sun sets. I pull into the parking lot of the grocery store with the broken out windows, and I back the open truck as close as I can to the entrance. I don't see any creatures, but I exit the truck resting my bow against my shoulder, just in case.

First stop is the canned fish and meat section. I grab one of the canvas bags from the front and fill it with as much as I can carry. Tuna, salmon, beef jerky, any kind of animal protein I can get my hands on. Better to have it on hand in case hunting is scarce, and the boy needs more than refried beans and canned tomatoes. I check the bottled and gallon water shelves already knowing they would be empty. I return to the truck and pile the bags into the front seat, shaking my hands out relieving them from the effort.

Rachel had been right about getting caught in that herd. If I had not found the two of them, they would have died. The restaurant is a good spot for now, but it is only a matter of time before we get caught in another herd like that. They are joining together, the ones that are not stuck repeatedly walking into the same corner in the middle of a city. There are thousands of them still out there, lost in the plains and wide open spaces, coalescing together like droplets of an oil slick.

I grab what I can from the camping section: sleeping bags, canned heat, battery powered lanterns. Tomorrow I will ask Rachel if they want to come with me since the city won't be safe for much longer. The safety window after a large horde is only about three days before they start to trickle back into the city. I put the truck in reverse and twist the steering wheel back towards the road, heading to the restaurant.

Arriving back, I spot a clutch of zombies surrounding the side of the building, blocking the door. I drop the engine into neutral. The sound of the truck could draw them away, but I have a better advantage to take them down if they don't know I am there. Six on one side and five on the other. Two more than I have arrows for.

Shit.

I grab my crossbow and roll down the window. I scoot my body up through the opening, sitting on the window's edge and leaning against the roof of the truck, pulling the crossbow out onto the roof. At this distance, I cannot tell what is happening inside the restaurant. The zombies all mill about, bumping into each other and the glass windows. I lean my crossbow across the top of the pickup, lining up my eye with the cross hairs.

I set the arrow and squeeze the trigger.

The first one goes down, tumbling like a bag of bones. I take aim again. The two nearest to me turn around at the sound of the arrow releasing. One shuffles towards me in that broken falling manner that reminds me of twisted tree branches. I line up my shot and squeeze the trigger again. The arrow flies through him creating a hole where his eye used to be, flying into the head of the one behind him. Two for one. It pays to practice, I guess.

The remaining creatures on the other side still just continue their mindless movements, skidding against the window, leaving smudges of skin and gore against the transparent panes. The constant banging and shuffling would be enough to drive a person mad.

I have seven arrows left, and I take down the next three. I ditch the crossbow in the truck before I pull myself the rest of the way out. My muscles burn as I lower my feet against the gravel, careful not to make a sound.

There still has not been any movement from inside the building, and my hope is that Rachel has enough faith in me that they are holed up in there as deep as they can get. I pull my knife out from my belt, taking sideways steps towards the first one, plunging my knife into the base of the first zombie's skull. The last one turns, its dead-white eyes focusing on me.

Facing only one of them has never been a problem, not that it would be. Just a quick blade to the head and that is that. This time though, something about my angle, the way the creature lunges, catches me off guard. It grabs a hold of my forearm just as I pull the knife out, giving me no leverage. Its teeth snap shut just inches from my arm. I stumble back trying to keep my exposed skin away from the gnashing teeth. Its fingers are nothing more than dead, grasping bones wrapped in flesh, and my stomach turns flip flops at the sensation.

The zombie's head explodes, leaving a smatter of brain and viscera on my shoulders. Now just a bloody stump, its body crumbles to the ground, fingers losing purchase on my skin. I see Rachel standing outside the door, lowering a shotgun. We make it inside and both turn to pull the booth back in front of the door as quickly as possible before I collapse against the staircase in the middle of the room.

"You okay?"

"Yeah, I'm fine. Marcus?" I ask.

"He's in the kitchen," she says as she lowers the shotgun to her side.

"Where did you find it?" I nudge my chin towards the weapon.

"I found it underneath the flour bins in the pantry."

"We have to relocate," I say as I catch my breath.

She raises her eyebrows towards me.

"The noise of the shotgun," I explain. "Loud sounds draw them."

"I didn't know that," she says with a flicker of regret in her expression.

"No matter," I say, standing. I found us a vehicle, a pickup truck."

"Oh, that's good." She smiles.

"It should be a good vehicle for us. I picked up supplies, too. We can take that gun, but we need to find some more weapons for the two of you."

"The two of us?"

"He needs to learn." I cannot look at her directly and I focus on a spot against the far wall.

She nods as another flicker of sorrow crosses her face. "How much more time do we have to get out of here?" she asks.

"That depends on how close they are. When did these show up? How long were they out there?"

"Since this morning, just after sunrise."

"That's what I was afraid of. We need to move quickly. Do

you still have the knife?"

She nods.

"Okay, give me a few minutes to gather my arrows. Then I'll get the truck and pull it as close to the door as possible to get you and Marcus inside. We have to assume that more are coming and that they could be here any second. If we circle back around in two or three days we should have an idea if it is safe to come back here."

"Right, okay." She nods, but her eyes trail off behind me to the kitchen.

I do my best to hide the frustration that she had shot the gun. A few more seconds and I could have taken him down, but as things are now we probably have less than an hour to get out of here, if that. I keep my face turned away from her focusing on getting everyone out as quick as possible.

Through the swinging doors, we find Marcus sitting in his nest of restaurant tablecloths underneath the prep table. He found a few kitchen utensils to playing with. He bobs them up and down, adding his own affected voice and giving character to his new found toys.

"It's time to go, Marcus," I say speaking in a light but firm voice . "Come and see the great blue truck I found for you."

"Really?" he says as he glances up, his expression lighting up.

"Yeah."

I turn back to Rachel. "The two of you need to stand ready at the door," I say. "I'm going to collect my arrows and bring in the truck. Keep watch and come out the front door as soon as I stop.

Okay?"

She nods, a quick short movement.

It only takes me a few minutes to pull the arrows from the heads of the inert creatures. The bone structure does not have the same sturdiness as a human. Once they transform over, the body starts to decay at the same rate. No one knows what reanimates them. Each arrow comes loose with a quick pull, but I have to place my foot on the shoulder of the last creature to get enough leverage to tug the arrow out.

Turning, I quickly scan the landscape looking for any kind of sign. The hilliness gives me a bad feeling. I much preferred the flatness of the landscape out west. If one can see for miles, a whole herd could be approaching and we would have hours of advanced notice. Here, they could come over the hilltops and we would have minutes at the most.

I pause, listening as hard as I can to the sounds around me.

There it is. In the far distance, I can just make out the shuffle and scrape indicating the incoming presence of zombies. I train my eyes on the truck sitting up the road about fifty yards away. The urge to run almost takes over, but I fight the impulse. If I step back inside we would all be trapped indefinitely, depending on how many there are. A sizable horde could get stuck, creating a wall around the building.

With a brisk but careful pace, I head towards the truck keeping along the side of the parking lot. I do not want to risk tripping in the thick grass by going directly up the hill. Once I make it to the road, I can see the adjacent valley facing out towards the outer edge of the city. I see them. Not as many as the original herd, but enough to potentially wrap around the restaurant as I feared. They shuffle along about twenty deep.

I trot towards the truck and swing into the driver's seat. Stealth is pointless. By now they already know I am here. My job is to get Rachel and Marcus into the truck and out of the immediate area. I rev the engine and pull forward into the parking lot until I see Rachel with Marcus hiding close behind her through the glass door. Her eyes dart between the truck and the front line of the herd now trickling over the slope fifty yards away. She nudges Marcus forward as I push the passenger door open. He scrambles the few feet into the truck, Rachel swinging in just after him.

As soon as she pulls the door shut behind her, the leading edge reaches the tailgate of the pickup truck. The engine guns and we surge forward. They have already blocked the way out of the parking lot as they continue to stream over the hilltop. I turn the wheel and press the gas, spinning the truck almost up on two wheels.

“What are you doing?” Rachel asks in a panic.

“I have to break through. It's the only way.”

“Are you sure?!”

“Just hold on tight.”

When I press down on the gas pedal, I keep my eyes trained on the tree on the other side of the road in an attempt to ignore the approaching herd. Twenty deep is still a significant number. Rachel pulls her seat belt across her chest and over Marcus' lap before she clicks it into the receiver between us. Her arm is wrapped tight around him; he clenches his eyes shut, burying his face into her arm.

I press my foot down on the gas pedal and plow through. The zombies bounce off the bumper and windshield like rubber, clutching feebly towards the windows as we surge past, their slick fingertips unable to grasp the metal surface as the truck pushes past them.

"We're okay," I say. "We're okay."

I have overshot the road but I straighten the car back to the pavement and we steady our way down the road back into town.

"You guys alright?" I ask.

"Yes," Rachel gasps.

Marcus' curiosity gets the best of him, and he wiggles out from under her arm, craning his head around. I press forward as the three of us fall into silence. We are safe for now, but we need to get to shelter. We are putting enough distance between us, and the zombies soon disappear behind us.

I glance over at Marcus who gazes out the window, wide-eyed and restless.

"I have an idea," I say. "Let's go and get some weapons, and then we'll do something fun."

"Something fun?" he says, scratching his nose.

"You'll see, but first things first."

I pull the truck up to what was once a sidewalk, as close to the building as possible. The windows have long since been broken out. "Wait here," I say. "I'll flush the place and then motion for the two of you."

I climb out of the truck slowly, holding my knife in one hand and my other resting on the hilt of my bow, I move into the building, careful to step over the broken glass. My first stop is the knives. I circle back and wave them inside.

Rachel picks up a few switchblades, eyeing the large glass case of throwing stars. She hands one of the knives to Marcus, who eyes it warily before he tucks it into his back pocket. I get lucky and find another cartridge of arrows; my brand even. I refill my arrow cache, noticing that I have not lost as many as I had in the past.

"I think there are less of them," I say.

"Now that you mention it, I think you are right." She stops and turns towards me, focusing on the empty road through the window behind me. "When it happened--whatever it was that made this happen--there were hundreds, if not thousands, of them. They were everywhere. But now, I don't think we've seen more than fifty this week, outside the occasional herd. I think they are going away from the cities."

I turn and face the same direction as her. The street is dusty. Waves of heat radiate off the pavement. "It wasn't always this way," I say. "The world was once alive and vibrant."

"Yeah," she says glancing over to Marcus, staring at a wall of flying discs, ignoring both of us.

"Maybe one day it will be again."

Marcus steps between us and the window, staring out, framed by broken glass and rotted wood. I walk up next to him and watch him try out the feel of his new knife. He flips it around in his hands, opening it and closing it, testing the edge of the blade against his thumb.

"Do you like it?" I ask.

"Yeah," he replies. I can tell he is hiding his excitement at finally having a weapon. The grin escaping the edge of his lips is a dead giveaway.

"Come on." I nod my head back towards the truck. Rachel falls in behind us in the pattern we have become accustomed to, with Marcus in the middle for the best protection.

We circle around the corner and down the block, once more pleasantly surprised by the lack of zombies in the area. Even just a few weeks ago they still lined the downtown area. The herd had cleared out quite a bit of them. I pull up to the place I want to show them, parking close and pointing to the revolving door of a large glass building, surrounded by a vacant, paved courtyard.

"In there?" Rachel asks.

"Shh," placing my finger over my lips. "Through the revolving door and then we will be safe. This building is clear. We'll be safe."

As soon as our feet hit the concrete we all sprint towards the door, pushing our way through in one segment of the revolving door.

"What is this place?" she asks, helping Marcus to his feet.

"It's a library," I reply.

They both look up into the huge four-story atrium in the center of the space. Hanging from the topmost level of the ceiling falls a thick wire the length of the building, ending in a large, brass-covered pendulum. It swings as if with a force of its own, over the fenced expanse, slowly moving from side to side. Other than the slight creak of the wire there are no other sounds.

"It is safe," I say, trying to calm their awed expressions. "I come here quite a bit when I do supply runs."

“What is that?” Marcus asks pointing to the device.

“That is called a Foucault pendulum. There is a great book about it just over there in the shelves.”

His face lights up and he gazes up at Rachel. She looks at me with a question in her eyes.

“The whole building is safe,” I say. “I've cleared it and secured all the doors. The only entrance is the revolving door and they can't maneuver it.”

“Stay where I can see you,” Rachel says to him before he trots off into the children's area to the left of the atrium. She turns to me. “How did you find this place? It's incredible.”

“I stumbled in here a couple of years ago, running from a herd. That courtyard in front used to be crawling with them. I came around the corner from the other direction on a supply run, but I got stuck. They surrounded me. I nearly fell into the revolving door. The building was empty. I spent some time strengthening the rest of the doors, but so far I have not seen any evidence that they can get through.”

“This place is amazing,” Rachel says as she begins to wander around. She steps into the shelving area, close to where Marcus sits cross-legged on the floor, flipping through the pile of books he has amassed next to him.

Rachel trails her fingers along the spines of the books, pausing over one and pulling it out from the others. It is a book I have read, about a little girl who lives on a farm, but pines for greater things. She gets swept away into another world where everything comes to life in vibrant color. I pull up one of the small stools and sit down, watching Rachel glancing through the pages with a distant smile playing on her lips.

I can tell by the voracity in which Marcus plows through the books that he has not had an opportunity like this for a very long time. He takes in every detail of the pages, carefully placing each book to the side after he finishes reading.

A flash of a lost memory returns to me. A bed, large and pink, piled with pillows and a quilted comforter. A few feet away is a painted white bookshelf filled to the brim with brightly colored spines.

"Are you alright?" Rachel asks.

"Yes." I blink and shake my head, laughing a little. "Just lost in thought. Oh, I almost forgot. There is one more thing I wanted to show you."

Rachel watches me with curiosity as I jog back to the small open cafe area. I climb over the counter and spot the boxes in the back storage room. Within a few minutes, I return with a handful of chocolate bars.

Rachel looks at me with disbelief.

"Candy doesn't go bad," I say. "Go on. Take it."

We all enjoyed our small respite while Rachel reads us a chapter. We all lounge in the small, brightly colored corner of the library pretending for just a few moments that we live in a different world. The sun hangs low to the horizon. We opt to set up camp on the second floor after pulling the supplies we needed from the truck.

We stay awake for a little while, feeling euphoric from the break in our reality. I have a nudge of a feeling that something is looming, but I push aside my sense of dread to enjoy the small company that we have formed. As dusk settles, Rachel reads to us until Marcus falls asleep, tucked into one of the sleeping bags I had retrieved. Once he is settled, she sits down across from me in one of the plush chairs, adjusting the light of the lantern on the table between us.

We talk for a little while. She tells me about the people she has lost, her husband, his parents, and then when they set out to escape the overrun city out west, the group they joined and then subsequently lost. It all sounds very complicated, yet there is also a strange comfort in hearing it. The battery powered lantern holds a steady glow. Even though she is telling me her past, I avoid giving her any information as much as I can. Rachel finally steps over to her sleeping bag and settles in. Soon her breathing grows steady and even.

I sit for another few moments, watching them both to ensure they have fallen asleep. I creep away, careful to step only on the carpeted part of the stairs to the level below. The books are inviting and welcoming. I trail my fingers over the smooth surface of the spines, lined up on the shelves. The area underneath the balcony is shielded in dark shadows. I find my way to the back wall, away from where the others are sleeping and out of view of the glass doors before I sit against the wall, pulling my knees up to my chest.

The tears come silent at first. The pressure of the day overtakes me and I cannot help but let it. I do not want to wake them. No matter. I have become accustomed to crying silently. The tears flow fast, falling off my chin and staining my clothes, my body racked with emotion. I stay this way, clutching my arms around me, turning to press my face against the wall. I cry myself out until I feel numb and there is nothing left. There is no comfort here or anywhere. Not for me, not for anyone. Not anymore.

Five

I wake before the others.

The sun filters through the windows creating a light orange glow on the surroundings. Sometime during the night I had come back upstairs and tucked into the sleeping bag left out for me. My first thought is to get back to the laboratory where I had found the photograph. Since the place had already triggered memories for me, I want to find out more. I sit up and rub my eyes as last night's dream rushes across my mind.

I was in a car hearing voices. A woman spoke in low hushed tones to the driver, a dark-skinned man from the laboratory.

"We have to get as far away as possible," she said.

The car moved fast, and I was unable to see over the edge of the window. I knew we are headed west and something bad had happened. The people in the car kept saying phrases like "We have to take care of Ashley." I remember feeling excited because I had never been outside the lab before.

We had driven for a long time when we came to a large crowd sprawled across the highway. There was something wrong with all of them. We did not know yet what had happened, that the people had changed into predators. We were surrounded all at once. The driver kept going as fast as he could. Despite the danger surrounding us, I wanted nothing more than to be able to see out the window.

I sit up in my sleeping bag, pressing away the remainder of the disturbing dream.. A sound catches my attention. A distant scratching. At first, I think it is the last remnants of my fading dream but soon realize it is not just my mind playing tricks. I do actually hear something. Rummaging through the supplies we managed to bring inside, I quickly find a baseball bat before heading back downstairs to the lower level of the atrium.

At first glance, I cannot guess how many there are, or how deep the layers go. There are dozens of them clawing at the glass entryway to the lobby. If the glass breaks, we are all trapped. If the others were not on a higher level there would be no hope, but I take small comfort in the knowledge that they are still upstairs. I know I can handle these before they get out of hand. Two of them have gotten caught inside the revolving door but they do not have the momentum to push the door forward. If I wanted to, I could just revolve it the other direction and kick them back out to the street.

I take a deep breath.

Pushing open the door, I allow them through as I clasp the bat in my right hand. The two stagger around me as I back up, careful to avoid the pendulum behind me. The movements of my body alert them of my presence, right in front of them. Fresh meat. They hold back but their teeth chatter as if in anticipation. Both of them hover around me, lurching in slow motion, dead eyes waiting for something, some move from me.

I give it to them. I circle the bat around for better leverage before I let it swing, making contact with the first one. His head knocks clean off and lands on the tile, sliding across with a sickening squelch before stopping in front of the cafe counter. I take the other one down with a quick knife jab to the side of the head.

It is far too easy.

They do not attack. I have seen them take down a person more times than I care to remember, enough for me to know I want nothing to do with them. I try to avoid it but, if I had to, I could walk through a crowded room of them if it came to it. I have no idea why.

Still, I avoid them, as I don't know what would happen if one of them bit me. If they outnumbered me I could still get trampled or injured. Either way, I fight them to keep up the camouflage for when I am around other people. If I seem different from anyone else it makes me a target.

I let in three more. In a strange way, it feels good to fight them one-on-one like this. It has been a while, and I don't like to be out of practice. Besides taking them down one at a time will help to diminish the horde pressed against the glass.

I feel glad of the presence of Rachel and Marcus, but something about the way he looks at her puts my teeth on edge. The utter devotion which only comes from a child. It is up to me to keep them safe. I have no illusions about that.

The creatures soon lay in a heap before the locked glass doors. I turn and watch the rest of them hammering at the transparent wall between us. I step up close to one as she presses her decaying face against the glass, snapping her teeth as if trying to bite her way through. Her dead eyes stare right through me. It would be easier to kill them if they had some kind of meanness about them, some kind of motivation behind their actions. But they just move forward until they come to something that stops them.

I decide to let a few more through the revolving door.

I reach forward to push the partition around, and I feel it come loose in my hand. Three more creatures had wedged between the other side and the door is stuck fast. Their movements, paired with the pressing herd behind them causes the center shaft to snap.

"Ash?"

Marcus' voice behind me startles me enough that I lose my footing. Swinging my head around, I see him standing in the middle of the steps watching me, his eyes wide.

"Get back!" I say through clenched teeth as I struggle to push the glass panes back, doing my best to keep them at bay.

It is too late. My feet slip out from under me on the slick marble floor. The glass cracks, and I fall backward, hard on my backside as the doors cave in like an umbrella turning inside out. Dozens of creatures surge through the breech, walking right past me towards Marcus. I spin around, landing on my elbows, straining through the shuffling legs to see if he has moved. I catch a glimpse of him darting around the corner at the top of the stairs. He may have a chance.

I crouch with my arms over my head to ward off the throngs of feet stepping over me, obscuring my vision as they flood the atrium. At this rate, the entire lower floor will soon be filled with them. When the movement slows, I stand. They adjust to my presence without acknowledging and a circle of space forms around me. They slow their motions, milling about, bumping into the walls and each other. When they wander close to me, they just veer off as if I am wearing some kind of zombie repellent.

When I step forward they part in front of me, allowing me a

path through the horde. If I engaged one or attacked them, they would turn on me, but as long as I move slowly they ignore my presence. They move out of the way each time I take a step. When I reach the stairs, I can see across the atrium that about a dozen have made it into the stacks, roaming up and down the aisles. I sprint up the stairs, two at a time. Marcus and Rachel are clutched in each other's arms, both staring at me with wide questioning eyes. At the top of the stairs, Rachel had seen everything.

"We have to move," I say pushing past, grabbing my sleeping bag and shoving it into the case.

"How did you do that?" Rachel asks.

"We'll talk about that later." I shove the beef jerky and the rest of the cans into the backpack, scanning over the edge of the balcony. "We have to move quickly if we have any chance of getting out."

"I saw you walk past them," she says evenly. "How did you do that?"

I keep my gaze steady as I turn back to her. She is panicking and her mind is focusing on the wrong thing right now.

"Okay, Rachel," I begin. "You are right. I did do that, and I'll be happy to tell you about it. But first, we need to get you and Marcus out of this building before too many of them get inside."

She nods. Her eyes flick towards Marcus as her rapid breathing evens out. "How are we going to get out of here?" she asks.

"There is a set of emergency stairs over by the elevator. We need to make it down them before too many of them get inside. I don't know how secure the door is and that is our only way out. Do you understand?”

“You can do it, right? You can walk right past them. You can get the car and crash through and come back for us?”

“That's not how it's going to happen.”

“Why not?”

“Because you think I will leave you both behind.”

She stares at me, jaws clenched, her arms draped protectively around Marcus' shoulders. I can tell by her expression that my guess is right.

“We go together or not at all,” I say as I reach my hand to her. She takes it and I feel her fingers trembling.

“What's the plan?” she asks in a quiet voice.

“I'll go down one flight in case I have to clear the area. Then I'll signal the two of you. The door opens out to the street. Then we'll have to make our way around the building to the truck. See the door there by the elevator?”

“Yes, I see it.”

“Through there are the stairs. It will be dark, but stay close and let me go first. It should be clear since the inner door should still be secure, but wait for my signal. Walk fast and steady. Whatever you do, don't run. We don't want anyone to panic. Understand?”

She nods. I meet eyes with Marcus, and he nods too. I notice a wicked determination on his face, something I have never seen before.

I reach for the crossbow, holding it up against the edge of the balcony and aiming with careful precision. Down below I notice two drawing close to the door leading to the exit. The arrows take them down, creating a macabre wall so none of the others can approach the door. I will lose those arrows, but it is a small price to pay.

"Okay," I say as I swing the bow to my back. "Ready?"

"Wait," Rachel says, her voice high and thin. "What happens when we get outside? Won't there be more of them?"

"They are coming from the west and if they do anything they do it in a straight line. The back of the building should be clear."

We do one last weapons check, nodding to each other. I can see the fear in her face, but she is holding strong. We approach the door, painted the same gray color as the wall around it. The long dead 'exit' sign hangs at a slant. I pull it open, keeping my bow down by my side. I step down the stairs doing my best to listen. All I can hear is the silence of the stale air and an occasional thump from the lower level. As soon as I make it to the first landing, I can see the door is cracked beneath me. Just enough to notice it is not latched.

I reach down, slip the knife out of the sheath at my ankle, hold it tightly as I move forward, motioning to them with my other hand. As they move down the stairs, I adjust my body to keep myself between them and the door. Keeping three steps ahead, I reach the door to the outside first and push it open with my forearms, all of us squinting at the light. Seeing the open door and the small square of sun cast upon the dusty floor kicks all of us forward, eager to get out of the claustrophobic surroundings.

One of the zombies from inside the library lurches against the door, pushing it further open. Marcus lets out a surprised yelp, immediately clasping his hands over his mouth realizing his mistake. All three of us burst into action, darting out the door. I push it closed behind us, but if the creatures breach the inner door, there are no guarantee it will hold.

"Go," I say gesturing them across the street.

I was right about the creatures not being behind the building. Now we just have to make our way around to find the truck. My hope is that we do not have to abandon it along with all the gear in the back. Besides, I like that truck. I cannot say that about many things.

We circle wide around the building, not crossing a single zombie until the sidewalk on the other side of the courtyard. I see the truck, the top of it at least. Parked along the edge of the sidewalk a few feet from that now broken glass wall, it is surrounded on all sides.

"It's not worth it," Rachel says. "We can find another vehicle."

"No," I reply. "I can get it. You two stay here. Get up on that fire escape until I get back to you. We don't have time to argue. Go!"

They scramble up to the first level as I walk forward. Once again the pathway parts before me allowing me several feet of room each time I take a step. With little effort I walk to the truck, slow and steady, open the driver's door and crawl in. The roar of the engine makes some of them turn my way and the ones nearest begin to grasp at the windows. They fall away as the truck nudges forward. I could have floored it, but I have experienced cleaning guts out of a grill before, a task I do not wish to repeat. Once I clear the edge of the horde, I surge forward aiming for the ladder of the fire escape. The truck lurches when I jump the curb.

Rachel and Marcus scurry down, clutching to the rungs as I back the bed underneath them. Rachel jumps down first, turning to help Marcus into the truck bed. She pulls him down and they both fall flat, burying themselves in the stash of goods. She taps her foot against the cab to signal me.

We surge forward and I cut the wheel, heading out of town. Within minutes, the buildings fall behind us into the distance.

I find a grassy area and pull over so they can climb up into the cab of the truck. Marcus' eyes glow and Rachel watches him with some trepidation. I think I know what she is thinking. The smirk on his face indicates that he is enjoying the adventure. He is enjoying himself far too much. I reach under the seat and pull out a large bag of beef jerky.

"This should tide us over, but we need to get somewhere to make camp," I say.

"Where do we go now?" Rachel asks.

"You said the two of you were headed east?"

"That's right."

"Then I guess we are heading east."

The two-lane highway is vacant before us. It takes several minutes but finally her features slowly fall into a relaxed smile.

Six

We drive in silence for a long while, the sun hanging lower in the sky behind us. Rachel keeps a wary eye on me while Marcus munches happily on his food. The countryside slips past outside the window.

"Why are you helping us?" Rachel asks, breaking the silence.

"What do you mean?"

"You obviously know your way around. You can survive on your own. That much is clear, but what I don't understand is why you would help us. It would be a lot quicker to go on your own without us. It is no secret that you have some other agenda, so why did you let us tag along? You could have just as easily left us back at the mansion."

I keep my eyes on the road, a gray two-lane, slicing through the trees. "I suppose you're right, but what would have happened if I had done that?"

"We would have died. I am sure of it."

I glance down at Marcus, unsure how to continue.

"This is the only world he has ever known, right?"

"Close to it. He was born shortly after the Fall."

"I think that a shameful truth," I say. "If there is some way he can one day see something different than all this... I don't care any more if I see that world, but it would be enough for me to know that someone will."

"What about you?" she asks after a moment.

"What about me, what?"

"What happened to you, your family?"

"I've been alone since I was eight," I begin. "I don't remember much before that, but we were driving and the car hit a tree." The memory is fresh, as it is one of the first true memories that I had. I had seen the driver here and there at the laboratory, but I did not know him personally.

"The creatures swarmed around us immediately," I say continuing the story to Rachel. "I hid in the back seat trying to keep as quiet as possible. I was unhurt by the accident but remained certain that my life would end within minutes.

"It took several minutes to realize they were gone. They had not touched me. They never have since then either, unless I get their attention first."

She does not answer, but keeps her gaze on me for several minutes before finally turning to face the road. We drive for a long while before we see another zombie. Just the one, wandering through the field at the side of the road. The sun dips behind the tree line and darkness falls. Finally the exhaustion takes over and Rachel volunteers to drive. As much as I hate to stop at night, we pull over at the next patch of road. We both circle around the front of the truck. Marcus sleeps undisturbed in the center seat. When I slide in, his head lolls over and lands against my shoulder.

The road drones on.

"How long have we been on the road?" Rachel asks.

"About six hours now, I think."

"Do you think a fire would be a bad idea once we stop?"

"It never has been a problem before," I say. "If anything, it keeps them away. I'll take the first watch though, just to be on the safe side."

"You don't have to. I can take it."

"It's okay. I caught some sleep while you were driving."

"You did?" she asks.

"I did," I fib. "I'll be fine."

We spend the next few hours collecting firewood, all of us staying within eyesight of each other. Once we return to camp, Rachel turns up a large stump to use as a stool arranging her gathered wood onto the firepit. She begins to rub two of the sticks together.

"Hang on," I say reaching into my backpack.

"No, I've done this before. When I was younger. It might take a bit but I can get it started this way."

"Here," I say with a grin as I toss her the lighter. "This might be quicker."

She catches it in midair. "This should help," she replies with a wry smile.

"You can keep that one," I say. "I've got several."

I sit with my back to the tree while the two of them settle in, wrapping up in their sleeping bags. Most of the gear has made it with us even though none of it was strapped down in the back of the truck. It takes me only a few minutes to circle the camp and find the best spot to keep watch. Sleeping outside is not ideal, but the fire should keep them away. The large tree on the northern end of the circle offers the best coverage. I place my bow down, stretching out my legs in preparation for the long stretch of sitting still.

The fire smolders a low amber beacon. The other two have fallen asleep, based on the steady sound of their breathing. The forest surrounds us with pitch darkness on all sides, tree trunks only illuminated by the dancing flickering light.

I hear a crack of branches in the underbrush.

My hand flies to the knife at my waist, and I roll forward into a crouch. The crossbow lays on the ground beside me. Another snap of a twig, a rustle of leaves. I bring my knife up, ready for the side slash which would take down an approaching zombie. What I hear next alerts me that this is not the usual shuffle of mindless movement. I slowly push myself to standing, hooking the strap of my bow over my shoulder and placing my hands against the tree.

It is close.

I hold my breath.

Another step.

I move forward as quiet as I can against the leafy ground, catching a glimpse of Rachel sleeping with her hands tucked under her cheeks, breathing softly. Marcus' bag is piled in a heap between me and the fire. Every muscle in my body is taut and alert. Whatever is moving through the forest stays in the darkness at the edges of the clearing. My eyes strain to try and make out the shape. It steps into the flickering light of the fire and I swing around with my knife at the ready.

Marcus peers up at me, his hair kicked up creating a rooster at the back of his head.

"What are you doing?" I whisper in an exhale, not without

some annoyance. I lean back against the tree and slide down to the ground.

"I couldn't sleep," he says with nonchalance, settling into the ground next to me. He pulls his feet up and looks at me in that unnerving way. I can't help but feel that he is watching me, as if I have something for him.

The darkness grows around us. "Fine," I say. "You can stay but you have to be quiet okay?"

He nods with a comfortable look on his face.

"You wanna know something?"

"What?" I say with a sigh.

"Our names are the same."

"Are they? How do you mean?"

"My middle name is Blaze."

"Really?"

"Yeah," he grins. "Marcus Blaze. We both have fire names. Pretty cool, huh?"

"I guess so."

He smiles and settles in, perching next to me as if we had done for years, instead of being near strangers, tossed together by circumstance.

"Marcus, did you need something?" I ask.

"I cry, too, sometimes," he says quietly.

"What?"

"I heard you yesterday in the library. I didn't want to say, but..."

"No, it's alright." I wave my hand, though it is not alright.

"It's okay, you know." He scoots over to me and picks up

my arm, draping it over his shoulder like a scarf. I sit in silence and let him lean in underneath the small comfort he seems to get from me. I cannot decide if I want to smile at him or if his presence makes my neck bristle.

Bolting awake, I immediately recognize the sound of the creatures moving through the trees, sunlight fingering through the branches. I had fallen asleep on my watch. Something about the presence of Marcus had lulled me into a relaxed state and I had nodded off. He sleeps with his head on my lap and his arms tucked around my waist.

I try, at first, to push him off. The zombies are close. I don't know where, but I can tell they are nearby. I twist around, catching a glimpse of Rachel still sleeping at the edge of the circle. If I can get her to wake up, we might be able to make a break for the truck before they spot us. Marcus' arms clutch around my waist in a sleep induced grip, his hands locked together.

"Marcus," I whisper through clenched teeth. "Marcus, you have to let go!"

I spot the first zombie step through the trees.

"Marcus," I say with urgency. "You have to let go. Rachel! Rachel!" I say over my shoulder as loud as I can while not giving away our position. If Marcus would just let go...

I kick out my feet and try to get some purchase against the tree to loosen his grip.

The zombie makes it to Rachel before I can. Seeing him hover over her gives me an extra surge of adrenaline. I shove Marcus off of me and toss him aside. As much as I hate it, I know it is our only chance. He stumbles back onto his backside with wide eyes, his mouth dropped open. I glance back over my shoulder.

It is too late for her.

The zombie chomps into her neck as she sleeps, severing her vocal cords and crushing her windpipe. She struggles for a moment, her feet spasming in a quick seizure as her nerves fight for one last grasp at life. She is gone in seconds. I know the wheezing of the air working through her broken trachea is a sound that will never leave me. Marcus' chest is hitching up and down and his face goes white.

Grabbing him by the hand, I bolt towards the truck. By now there is no time to go back and gather the supplies. We make it as far as the passenger door. The herd filters around us, moving slowly through the trees, one at a time. I turn and see them lurching in slow motion, step after step. I yank the handle, but the door is stuck.

"Come on!" I mutter as they move closer, shuffling in behind us. Marcus begins to hyperventilate, clutching one hand in mine and craning his head around to see their steady approach.

"Don't look, Marcus," I say. "Don't look at them. Let me get the door open."

I run around the truck, letting go of his hand, thinking I can move faster, get him inside faster, if I go on my own. Lunging through the driver's side, I scramble across to push open the other door. He stands for a moment framed in the flaked blue painted door frame. Everything moves in slow motion. I reach for him, my hands clutching into thin air as I attempt to grab his shoulders and pull him inside.

I am too late.

He screams as the monstrous hands and fingers wrap around his arms and start to pull him away. I manage to get a hold of his wrists, but he slips away in seconds. They drag him into the forest as the sound of his wails echo into the night sky. The last thing I see are his hands clasping towards me, vanishing into the darkness of the forest.

No time.

No time to think. Even if they can not kill me, I could still get injured because of them. That many of them could overturn the truck. I scramble forward, grabbing the passenger door and pulling it shut.

"Come on," I mutter, willing the truck to move. "Come on!"

At last, the keys turn under my fingers, bringing the truck to life. The engine turns over with a disgruntled rumble. The roar of the engine grabs the attention of the creatures close to me. I find the road, pulling the wheel into position to get myself turned on the gravel. I drive until I hit pavement, leaving the creatures behind. I press the palms of my hands against my cheeks, wiping away the tears and doing my best to focus on the pressure of my foot against the gas pedal.

This had happened before, and yet...

He was a child. Marcus was a child.

I drive as far as I can, ignoring the nagging urge to circle back to the city and examine more evidence in the laboratory. All I want to do is move forward. It hurts now. Such a loss always does, but if I can just get enough distance between myself and what happened then maybe, just maybe, everything will be okay.

So many questions bubble in my mind, but I try not to focus on that. Despite my attempts to avoid the image, I play it over again in my mind. If I could have gotten her awake I could have prevented the whole thing. I could have saved him, saved them both. The sound of his screams would echo in my mind for the rest of my life. How many times, I wonder, do I have to live through the pain of seeing someone I care about, someone I loved, being ripped to shreds? I have seen enough of that to last a lifetime. Should have known better than to believe that this time would turn out any different. I swipe the back of my hand across my face then rub the wetness of my tears onto my jeans.

Pressing forward, the city fades into the distance. I have no destination in mind. The sun casts a yellow glow on the road. Hunger gnaws at my stomach, but it is a welcome distraction from the thoughts churning in my head. I need to find food and soon. At the next exit I pull off, motivated by the green road signs with invitations to Mom's Diner, Pete's BBQ, trucks welcome and so on.

The scent of grilling meat piques my interest as I turn the truck down the off ramp. I pull over in the parking lot of an abandoned grocery store. The light is fading fast, and I am hell-bent on finding where the scent of roasting meat is coming from. Stepping out of the cab, I lift my face to the wind, turning to catch the breeze. Finally I see it. Against the far northern horizon, rising from the treetops, is a thick gray plume of smoke dancing into the sky. Climbing back into the truck, I shift gears, pulling the wheel back onto the road.

Seven

The truck lurches forward. My focus remains steady on the gray beacon, the pillar of smoke rising from the tree-topped horizon. My cheeks feel sticky with drying tears. Pulling around to the main road, twisting the steering wheel with some effort, a sign comes into view, hand painted on bare wood with a red arrow pointing ahead.

"Food and Safety"

The prior tragedies of the death of my travel mates tuck themselves away in my mind, overtaken by the immediate desire to survive. The hunger gnaws at my stomach and can no longer be ignored. Up ahead I see another nearly identical sign with the arrow pointing to the gravel road off to the right. Forest surrounds me on all sides. At least I see no zombies in sight. I continue on following the tantalizing scent of food.

The road arrives to an open gravel circle, large enough for four of my trucks to park side by side. Up ahead, a metal fence topped with rolls of silvery barbed wire circles the expanse of property, vanishing into the forest on either side. A simple farmhouse nestles into the crook of the meadow. Behind the house is a warehouse and a sizable smoker, puttering along next to a huge fire pit, the source of the beacon which drew me to this place. The porch wrapping around the wooden sided house stretches across the front and sides of the building.

The scent of the cooking meat makes me feel weak with hunger.

I step out of the truck and approach the gate, trying to find a way to enter. The gate is locked with thick chains padlocked together. My eyes focus as I approach, allowing me to see the second layer of fencing creating a moat of sorts, an expanse of land acting as a buffer in case the outer fence becomes compromised.

A man emerges from the back of the house, following the path leading through the grass and towards the gate. He walks with purpose, even as he lifts his leg in an uneven gait. The limp is not enough to slow his approach. In his hands, he carries an old fashioned shotgun in a loose grip across his torso.

"What's your name, there?" he calls. His mustache bobs up and down as he speaks, rendering his mouth nearly invisible. He speaks in a relaxed, matter-of-fact drawl. If not for the shotgun, he would almost seem friendly.

"Ash Donovan," I reply.

"You got any weapons, Ash Donovan?"

"I have a crossbow inside the truck," I say, knowing better than to try and lie to him. "I also have a couple of knives. One in my belt and another at my ankles."

"Here's what'll happen, 'kay? I'm a goin' ta open both gates, you can go ahead and drive through. We'll leave your truck parked right here. But we're going to do everything real slow like so there's no funny business with that crossbow, ya hear?"

"I don't intend any funny business, sir," I reply.

He nods and gives a half wave, nothing more than a lift of his fingers from the hand wrapped around the butt of his shotgun. I climb back into my truck, rolling down the window before placing my hands back in view on the top of the steering wheel. Both gates are open and I pull forward. Through the rear view mirror, he closes the gates and returns to the window.

“If you don't mind, would you come out of your truck there, slowly. I'd like you to keep your hands in sight if you don't have any particulars.”

I do not have any particulars, and I do as he says. Not without a pang of regret, I pull the knife from the holster at my calf and the one at my waist and place it on the ground between us. His fingers twitch but he does not change the position of his hands on the gun. His expression is one of bemusement.

“That it?” he asks in a slow drawl.

“Yes, sir.”

“Be alright to leave the truck here. It's the safest place for now, and Eden'll have one of the boys drive it over to the lot. It'd be safe enough.”

“May I bring my backpack?” I ask.

“Got any weapons in it?”

“No sir, you can look if you need to.”

“No need,” he shrugs, shifting his feet. “Figure if you'd want to kill me you'da done it already. I reckon you'll be alright.”

He nods towards the house and I walk along the worn trail through the grass while he follows in step behind me. The farm resembles something from the cover of the old magazine at the library. The open meadow slopes off to the right where the forest creates a thick dark line. The footpath threads around to the back of the house.

“Eden will getcha fed,” he says as we trudge forward. “Seems like we get a new one every time we fire up that grill.”

I remain silent as we approach the house. The orange wood

siding emits a vibrant forest-y scent. We step up onto the blue-painted porch and he reaches around to open the screen door, gesturing me inside. A silver-haired woman, plump and smiling, emerges from the recesses of the house, drying her hands on a red checkered kitchen towel.

"Oh, Abraham!" she chides. "Put that gun down, now! She's nearly starving, to look at her!" She pulls out a chair and extends her generous arm out towards me. "Come in child, and sit down here. Let me make you a plate."

She bustles into the kitchen, her long skirt swishing as she moves. A combination of delectable scents waft towards me through the arch leading to the kitchen. I spot an open screen door, revealing the corner of the metal smoker.

My knees give out.

Abraham catches me underneath my arms, taking my backpack from me and setting it down in the foyer.

"I'm okay," I say, but my voice sounds weak, even to me.

"Here now, here now," he murmurs as he leads me over to the table. "A bite will do you some good now."

Eden, returns from the kitchen with a plate full of food, placing it on the table before me. Layers of roasting meat lying in a pool of thick brown gravy, roasted carrots and potatoes alongside. Specks of herbs and seasoning swim in the juices. I barely notice when she returns with an open jar full of cool clear water.

Instinct takes over. The fork is nothing more than a receptacle to bring the food, bite after bite, into my mouth. The flavor and abundance makes me feel as if I stumbled upon a feast. My truck and crossbow are fair trade for a meal such as this.

Neither of them speak as I eat. Eden moves around with serenity, fully aware of every detail of her surroundings. Her broad stance and relaxed shoulders emit the confidence of leadership.

"What will you do with my weapons?" I ask. "And my truck?"

"Don't worry about that right now," she says with a smile, her hands crossed in front of her. "You have been through it, haven't you? You poor thing. Let's get you rested first. There is plenty of time, and we have a room open for you."

"What is this place?" I ask, chewing the soft potato.

"Just know that you are safe," Eden replies. "We have plenty of food and water. You look like a stiff wind would have knocked you over out there." She sits down across from me, leaning her elbows on the table and glancing between me and the man she called Abraham. "Here is how it works here. We have many people come and go from this place. All are welcome here. You can stay for as long as you need to, to build your health back."

"Thank you."

"While you are here, however, you will be expected to contribute."

"Of course."

"You needn't worry about your weapons, either. They will be put into storage. You may have them back should you decide to leave the homestead for any reason. Sometimes we train and you may have them then as well, depending on the need."

As she speaks, the effects of the full meal after three days begins to creep up on me. Her words sound distant and her smiling face appears as if at the end of a long, dark tunnel. She stands and takes my arm, leading me down the hallway. The details escape me but we walk past many identical doors, some standing open, through which I see disheveled rooms, tossed clothing and open books. Evidence of life.

"Here," she says opening the door at the end of the hall. "It locks from the inside. I know how important it is to feel safe in a world such as this."

The bed is the only thing I see, a towering ordeal, draped with a white canopy over the four posts, piles of pillows in pristine cotton. Four grown people could have slept in such a bed with room to spare. It is the most beautiful bed I have ever seen in my life. Eden closes the door, a smile playing on her lips as she leaves me to my sanctuary. I manage to kick off my boots, but I have no memory of climbing the rest of the way into the blankets and the steep bank of pillows. Awareness is gone and I sink into the blissful darkness of sleep.

The food in this place is more than anyone could ever hope for. Mornings consist of eggs harvested from the chicken coop, smoke cured bacon from the room in the back of the warehouse, and any number of fruit preserves which they had put into storage during the time they refer to as the 'preparation years'. Eden has a gift for creating meals out of the little they have left. For example, after a day of roasted chicken, the bones are boiled into a broth. She whips up a batch of dough for dumplings and biscuits which lasts for a week.

Everyone had steered clear of me at first, but I sense now that my time of being the new girl is coming to an end. The young man next to me peers over, gnawing a bit of fat tucked in his cheek. He is not much more than a boy, maybe three years older than me with sandy blond hair and a smattering of freckles across his nose.

"Tell us a bit about yourself," Eden says at the table after the third day.

I offer a tentative smile but turn my eyes back to my plate. There are six children. Seven, including myself. They had all been here quite some time, guessing from their pink cheeks and bright eyes. The only one who seems out of place is the other girl at the end of the table, with dark, shifty eyes. We have passed in the hallway but have not spoken yet. I try to catch her gaze but she glances away each time, just like I would if someone were scoping me out. It takes me a few moment to realize everyone is waiting for my response.

"Oh...um..." I say, my voice sounding timid and small, even to myself. This is the most I have spoken in three days. "I was traveling and saw the smoke. I thought there might be people so I followed it to see what I could find."

"You smelled the food is more like it," the young man next to me chides with a grin.

"Now, Ezekiel," Eden says with a smile. "You are one to talk. Isn't that your third plateful?"

The others snicker and cover grins with their palms.

"So, Ash," she continues. "You carried with you some pretty strong knives and a hefty crossbow with you. Do you think you might be willing to teach the rest of us some of your weapons skills?"

The thought of getting my crossbow back is enough to make me agree to almost anything, but I keep my expression neutral, placing my fork carefully back on the plate. "I could do that."

"Wonderful!" she exclaims, clapping her hands together. "Many of us have lost our edge being within the safety of our home here. You must be very cunning to survive all that time out there on your own."

I catch sight of Ezekiel glaring at me suddenly. I keep his gaze, taking another bite as I do so. "No more so than anyone else."

"Did you have a family?" Eden asked. "You must have been young when the Fall happened."

"I was eight."

"I see." The room falls strangely silent. "And what became of them, your family?" Every eye at the table watches me.

"They died, early on. A riot. I've been on my own ever since."

She clasps her hands to her heart, "Oh, you poor dear."

"I guess it was fortune which brought me to your door," I say.

"Yes, yes. Indeed it was." She stands and begins to clear the plates, stacking them on top of each other before whisking them away to the kitchen. "Well, we are certainly glad you are here. Aren't we, Ezekiel?"

She gives him a pointed stare until he nods, slumping back in his chair. I sense another twitter of laughter behind everyone else's hidden expressions.

"I want to pair you two together today for the garden. Ezekiel will show you how to gather and get you acquainted with the process."

After the dishes are washed, we all filter out to the garden. Ezekiel gives me a surly look over his shoulder and motions to the row next to him. I kneel down facing towards him and begin pulling up the carrots buried deep in the ground, doing my best to copy his movements. On either side of us, the other children find their spaces, moving with care and skill. Eden walks among us, her hands clasped together as she peers over our progress. I glance over to my partner, turned away from me and yanking at the carrot tops.

"Your name is Ezekiel?" I ask in a low voice.

He nods.

"How long have you been here? At this homestead?"

"Since the beginning," he says. "Eden is my mother."

"Oh," I reply, pausing to take extra care with one carrot giving me difficulty. It gives way and I fall backward onto my backside in the moist earth. I try to laugh a bit, but he offers me nothing more than a scowl. Returning to his row, he continues forward.

"You will be 'teaching us', she said?" He spits the words as if the thought offends him in some way. I remain silent as I realize he is not asking me in search of a response. "What do you possibly think you could teach us? It was you, and people like you, who thought we were crazy. Just like the ark. Everyone scoffed, but we turned out to be right after all. Maybe it wasn't what everyone thought it would be, but it came to an end just like we said."

With every word, he yanked harder on each carrot, tossing them vehemently towards the patch of ground between us.

"Do you remember," I ask, "When things changed? When everything went bad?"

"Yes, I do." His eyes grow distant and he pauses, gazing out into the forest. "We prepared the garden, and the storage house over there. Enough for years to come. The only thing they did not foresee is them growing old, Mom and Dad. They needed people to help them. Tell me, Ash. How did you come to find this place?"

"What do you mean?"

"I mean," he pauses and faces me, leaning onto his knees, "this place is hidden behind a forest, off the main roads, not close to any big cities. How did you find your way here?"

This is a test. By the sidelong glance he gives, he knows quite well how I found this place. He wants to know if I will tell him the truth.

"You had it right," I reply. "It was the food. The smell of the food lured me to this place."

He watches me with a clear suspicion, nodding before speaking again. "It is always the food. That was Abraham's idea."

The matter drops and we continue down our row, leaving behind us piles of carrots which we will collect on the return trip. Deep in my gut I want desperately to ask more questions, to find out what this place is. Having a meal and a safe harbor is not an indicator of trust.

"Do you think you can teach us something we don't already know?" he asks after a long while.

"No, I don't. I've just been out there trying to survive, just like everyone else. But if I do have something to teach you, is there any reason why I shouldn't?"

He drops a carrot into the nearest pile, black dirt caked around his nails. Without looking at me, he stands and stalks away, leaving me in confusion. Wiping the sweat from my forehead, I watch some of the others talking and laughing, passing the time with each other as they gather the vegetables in their row. Ezekiel grabs the bucket and tosses the carrots into it, giving me the obvious cold shoulder as he passes me by.

"Hey," the dark-eyed girl calls out to me. "Let's go get some water. It's time for a break anyway."

"What is your name?" I ask, after walking over towards the others.

"Alma," she says.

We approach the edge of the forest, just inside the tree line. The double fence curves from the outer edge of the meadow in between the thick trees. The others each have a small bottle strapped to their hips and they take turns filling it under the silver stream dripping off the edge of the rocks. The water trickles down into a small cove in the ground underneath the fence.

"Here," Alma says as she hands me her bottle. It tastes cold and sweet, providing an instant relief when it touches my parched mouth. One of the other boys, Travis I think, shares his bottle with her.

"How long have you been here?" I ask.

"I've only been here a couple of weeks," she says, "but it's a good gig here."

"What do you mean?"

“I mean, they are legit, Eden and Abraham. Do your part and you will always have plenty to eat.”

She turns back and Travis drapes his arm around her shoulder. Everyone meanders back to the garden, returning to their tasks with languid commitment. I have never before witnessed this kind of behavior. Out there, people move quick with animal awareness. The people within this haven have grown accustomed to the reality of safety. Knowing they don't have to watch every corner to see if a herd of zombies might appear. I still jump at shadows. Perhaps I always will. Yes, the people here are nice for the most part, but I feel a sense of unease, nothing I can put my finger on, save for Ezekiel. At least, Alma seems nice.

Eight

"Hey. It's time to wake up."

A gentle hand nudges my shoulder, but I turn my face into the pillow, unwilling to acknowledge the day. Each morning there is a brief moment in which I forget where I am. Today is no different, but I cling to the details creeping into my conscience, one by one. The softness of the bed, the sensation of the girl perched at the edge of the bed jabbing at my shoulder. Already the fresh scent of outside lingers on her clothing.

"Go away, Alma," I mutter.

She hops to her feet, no doubt pleased at my waking. "We've got about an hour before breakfast. You don't want to miss it. Eden's killed one of the piglets so it's fresh bacon for us today!"

Alma plunks down in the armchair next to the brightly painted bookshelf. "Abraham is smoking again today," she says.

"What does that mean?" I sit up and rub my eyes with the heels of my hands.

"It means by the end of the day, there might be another person. These days it's pretty regular."

"Is that how you got here?"

"No." She laughs, a sound both sharp and light all at once. "Ezekiel found us during one of his supply runs. This is the last stop for many people before heading over the mountains."

"What is over the mountains, anyway?" I ask. In the three weeks I had been here, I keep hearing repeated reference to 'over the mountains', and I recall Rachel's desire to go East to the coast.

"They say there are no Z's there. People starting over.

That's the word anyway. This place is just a stopover for many trying to get there."

Through the window, the jagged horizon juts into the gray sky. So far I have stayed quiet listening to everyone around me, paying attention to Eden and how she watches over us, her wayward brood of lost orphans.

"Why don't you go?" I ask, tossing the thick blanket aside and standing up, arcing my arms overhead. "Over the mountains, I mean."

"Why would I? Everything I need is here. Travis is happy here too. We can help with the garden and upkeep of the land. As long as the fence holds up, we have no reason to move on."

"I see."

"Besides, they might be escaping the Z's but there is also the rogues."

"Rogues?"

"The mountain people, just out of reach of the Z's but living off the poor souls they catch traveling over to the East. They steal what they can and live off the land."

"If they live in the mountains, why don't they go on over to the coast?"

She shrugs. "Some people just have to take, I guess. Come on. You're going to miss out on all the bacon."

"Go on." I toss a ruffled pillow in her direction.

She laughs and disappears out the door. Other footsteps patter down the hall following the tantalizing scent of sizzling pork already drifting through the house. With the blue flannel robe wrapped around me, I peer out and trudge down to the closet room, an entire bedroom filled with a variety of clothing, jeans, flannel shirts, all added to each time they come back from a raid. Eden keeps the clothing for those who come through, often times in desperate need of a new set of threads.

After I dress, I head to the dining table, clean and refreshed, a feeling I am still trying to get used to. The atmosphere at breakfast is one of excitement. Everyone chatters among themselves, bright eyed, about what firing up the smoker means to the homestead. Eden steps in from the kitchen placing a platter of bacon in the center of the table, alongside the biscuits, followed closely by a large bowl of scrambled eggs. The chatter dissipates as everyone fills their plates, settling into the food.

"Ash, this is your first time through a smoker day," Eden says. "The others will have to walk you through it."

"What's different about it?" I sop up a bit of grease with my biscuit.

"Everyone gets the day off," says Ezekiel who has warmed to me in the last weeks.

"We're going up to the peak at the far edge of the forest," says Travis. "You should come."

"Okay," I reply. Alma keeps her eyes on me for several moments, stripped of emotion, before returning her attention to her eggs.

"That's where we first saw you, you know," Ezekiel says. "We spotted your truck coming down the highway on the west side of the valley when we were cleaning the spikes."

"Cleaning the spikes?" I ask.

"Ew," Alma exclaims. "Can we please not talk about that

until breakfast is over?"

"Yes," says Eden. "That would be best. Perhaps while you are up there you can show Ash how it's done. Now everyone needs to finish up, and don't forget to wash up your dishes before going out."

The platters before us are nothing more than empty pools of grease and morsels. Ezekiel and the others bound through the kitchen, leaving more water on the floor than in the sink. Alma stands at the door with her arms crossed, waiting and watching with narrow eyes. I drain the last of the milk in my jar before I join her, and we trot across the porch and out towards the warehouse.

The others arrive behind us and Alma passes out the water-filled canteens and a knife for each of us for our trek through the forest. Of the seven of us, Alma and I still held a natural distrust of the world around us, despite our growing comfort levels. Travis had acclimated more quickly, she had told me.

"So what's all this about cleaning the spikes?" I ask, catching up to her at the front of the pack.

"On the western edge of the property, there is an extra layer to the border fence."

Ezekiel pushes up between us. "They never suspected everything would go down the way it did. But after the Fall, that edge had the most of them coming in. After about the third time of rebuilding the fence, they decided to just create another level of security." He grins.

"Spikes," Alma continues. "Buried into the ground. Huge wooden logs, sharpened to a point and facing outward. It's a bit macabre, but it did the trick apparently. The only drawback is, every once in awhile, we have to go and remove the zombies. It won't take long, though. They say there are less of them now than there used to be."

We walk for a while without speaking. Without the threat of zombie hordes around each tree trunk I realize, perhaps for the first time, how beautiful and peaceful the forest is. The pine needles scent the air with a pungent aroma. The sunlight drifting through the branches creates an intricate pattern on the ground. We follow the path winding through the trees until it runs alongside the fence extending through the forest.

A sudden silence descends around us. This can only mean one thing. Zombies. Somewhere close. The forest feels eerie without a single bird or scurry through the underbrush. Even the wind has gone still.

"Wait," I whisper, motioning to the others. "Do you hear that?"

"I don't hear anything," Alma whispers.

"Exactly."

Ezekiel motions us quiet, adding in an eye roll for good measure. "That's because we are close to the fence. The spikes are up ahead. Come on."

We move forward with a solemn caution. Spotting them through the branches, I reach for the knife at my belt. My gaze darts towards Alma who seems frustratingly relaxed. She looks up ahead between the trees, stepping forward and motioning for us to follow. One by one, the others take out their knives.

The creatures are tangled against the fencing, three of them. Their feet step in place, struggling to move. The large spikes, roughly cut tree trunks, jut out of the ground at an angle and extend outward down the length of the fence from our location. The creatures make ghastly wheezing noises, low growls breaking the silence of the abandoned forest. Arms and legs flail, trying to move forward but hindered by the spikes jutting through their bloody torsos. However, the grizzly sound is not all I hear. Beyond the silence, the scrape of shuffling feet against the ground approaches through the trees. It is difficult to know how many.

Ezekiel turns with a grin on his face and a flash in his eye. He jogs down the length of the fence until he arrives at one of the gates leading to the space between the fencing. The others follow, and I bring up the rear, unsure of what is to come next. The six of them snake through the gate, doubling back. There is another gate on the outer layer of the fencing where they all gather. Ezekiel reaches for the handle.

"Wait!" I call.

Everyone turns towards me and I realize they cannot hear what I can hear.

"Let me do it," I say.

"Why?" Alma says.

"I have been out there most recently. I can handle them."

"We've been doing this for years," Ezekiel says. "Besides, there are only three of them. I think we got this."

"There are more coming," I say.

"Even more reason why we should get these down and get out of the way," he says, but a flicker of doubt drifts across his eyes. He pulls open the gate, the clank of the metal echoing through the trees. Ezekiel, Alma, and Travis move through the wall. The others hang back, knives ready and waiting to see if they are needed. The three of them each go to one of the struggling creatures. A quick jab in the temple and their bodies fall limp.

Branches snapping, twigs breaking.

We filter through the gate, everyone moving forward to lift the zombies off the spikes one by one. About five yards away is a large fire pit, and I realize right away what the purpose of it is. Everyone moves with lithe quickness, struggling little to lift the dead body weight off the spikes and dragging them across the ground to the pit.

They arrive from the left, a different direction than expected. Twenty of them descend upon us, appearing from between the trees, gruesome specters of what was once human.

"Get back now!" Ezekiel screams, the panic evident in his voice. He motions for everyone to get inside the fence. Travis stumbles, his foot catching on an errant tree root. Alma screams, whipping back to try and get him back to his feet. He struggles and collapses onto the ground, revealing an injured ankle. The creatures descend, right on top of them. Alma wraps her arms around his shoulders and they both squeeze their eyes shut, waiting for the inevitable.

"Come on!" Ezekiel calls, holding the gate. "There's no time!"

I grab Alma's knife, cast aside on the forest floor and leap forward, planting my feet between the two of them and the approaching monsters.

"What are you doing?!" Ezekiel yells. "Come on! We have to leave them!"

I concentrate, focusing. *Please let this work.*

The zombies slow their approach, one stands face to face with me. The others come to a complete stop. Behind me, Alma scrambles to lift Travis to his feet. Together they limp quickly, not stopping until they collapse within the inner wall, surrounded by the others. Ezekiel is the only one left, still holding the gate.

The one in front of me is close, too close. Its teeth clack together, a flap of skin hangs over one eye, edged in black rot. The flesh at the base of its neck gives a slight spongy resistance as my knife plunges through. I press my teeth over my lower lip, hoping to distract myself from the nausea.

I run. Ezekiel pulls me through the gate before slamming it shut. We both scramble towards the inner gate. Once safe, all seven of us watch in silence as the rest of the clutch wanders on, veering just past the spikes, shuffling aimlessly through the forest, undisturbed.

"You two head back to the farm," Ezekiel says jutting his chin towards Alma and Travis. "The rest of you head on up to the peak. We'll catch up with you."

They leave, Alma supporting her boyfriend's weight as they slowly make their way back down the dirt path.

"What was that?" Ezekiel asks. Already the sound of birds chirping returns to the surrounding atmosphere. I stand up from where I fell and dust the grass and dirt off my clothing.

"What was what?" I ask.

He stands up and faces me, the knife still dangling loosely between his fingers.

"I asked you a question."

“So you did,” I reply. I turn my back to him, facing out toward the fire pit where the slain zombies lay in a pile waiting for cremation. “What's going to happen to them.”

“We'll handle them later,” he says.

“I can't always make it happen,” I say keeping my back to him. “But they avoid me most of the time. I still have to be careful because I don't know what would happen if I get bit.”

“What does it feel like? What you did just there.”

His question evokes the uncomfortable feeling of connection, the same skin-crawling evocation one gets when touching an insect, only about ten times worse. I close my eyes. “You don't want to know.”

He does not speak. I hear him moving around behind me and for a moment I think he is going to kill me, leaving me piled with the others and hidden by the consuming flames. The forest is teeming with sounds. Crickets, birds, rodents scouring the underbrush. Finally, he walks back through the gate, heading towards the fire pit. He gathers wood from the nearby pile, burying the creatures. Without a word, I walk over and help him.

In the small clearing, we spend the rest of the afternoon building the fire until it soars, flames lapping upwards through the opening in the treetops. The bodies crackle and wilt like paper in the heat of the flames. Ezekiel avoids looking at me, but he motions now and then to an area which needs another log. At last, we walk back to the homestead.

“Ezekiel,” I say as we crest the hill.

“Yeah.”

“Do you think you could keep this between us? What

happened back there, I mean." The question is asked, though already I know better.

He nods after a moment. "Everyone saw it, though," he says. "I can't say so for them."

"It's all right. I think they have enough to worry about, with the excitement of the smoker bringing in new people and Travis' ankle. Maybe they didn't notice."

"Right," Ezekiel says. "Maybe."

Back in my room, I sense immediately something is off. The others are not back yet and Ezekiel vanished into the kitchen as soon as we entered. Already, a meal is underway in case the plume of smoke beckons anyone. I stand with my back to the door for a good long while, watching, letting my gaze roam over the details of the room. Nothing has changed, and yet...

My senses hone in, seeking and examining the details around me. Taking in the bookcase, the lay of the blankets, the way the chair is angled just so between the window and the shelf. The scent of the air, strange and lingering, shifting as if someone had just walked by.

The backpack.

Sitting where I left it at the foot of the bed, the dark fabric crumbled over itself, like a wrinkled old man sleeping under a tree. The satchel is clasped on the second hole. Thousands of miles I have traveled over the landscape of this country, the backpack has stayed with me all the while, keeping at least a day's worth of water and things collected over time. I know this backpack as well as I know any part of myself. And as sure as I breathe, I have always latched it on the third hole.

Landing on my knees in front of it, I scramble to open it, checking the pockets with a nervous caution. Everything is there. The red bandanna from a fallen friend, the stretch of fabric from the blue truck, the photograph of thirty smiling children standing in three rows next to an equally smiling adult woman. With growing panic, I check each pocket once more. The water bottle, the sanitary napkins, the extra knife blade, all there.

The picture from the laboratory is missing.

The photograph of the woman in the white coat. It is gone.

The rush of fury and sick rising in my stomach clouds my judgment. I take a breath, trying to focus my mind. After my heart returns as close to normal as I can get it, I return to the hallway with the goal to find Eden. From Travis' room I hear the lazy voices of him and Alma, catching a glimpse of his foot propped up on a tower of pillows.

Further down, Eden's bedroom door stands slightly open. I must tell her someone has taken something from my room. The open road is dangerous in many ways, but at least out there, I know the danger. Being here, surrounded by subterfuge, this is a different kind of danger. I creep down the hall and wait at the edge of her door, steeling my nerves. What stops me from knocking is the sound of her voice, trailing out from inside the room.

"I am certain of it," she says. "It is her. There is no doubt."

Peering around the corner, doing my best to stay out of sight, I glimpse her, shoulders slumped forward with her back towards me. I hold my breath and crane my neck around the doorway. She holds an object in front of her, a box with a coiled wire extending to a device held to her ear. What she holds in her other hand makes my blood run cold.

The photograph.

Eden speaks, unaware of my presence.

"I don't know yet how much control she has," she says. "But I am certain of her identity. There is a photograph placing her there.... Yes, yes! Right here in my hand.... Yes, of course...... Do you think it wise?"

The screen door slams shut as the others return, all jabbering about the couple they spotted coming down the road, following the plume. The afternoon's incident seemed all but forgotten.

"I think they have a baby with them!"

"It was just a bundle. Not a baby."

"I swear I saw it move!"

"You two quit squabbling. We'll see when they arrive at the gate. Someone tell Abraham!"

I stay back, ducking into the bathroom as they run by. They ignore me casually returning to my room. Immediately, A few of the books from the shelf go into the backpack as well. I'll have to stay down, and stay quiet. I will leave after nightfall.

The dinner before me is a combination of roasted meat, succulent, falling apart under the pressure of the fork. Gravy and homemade egg noodles. I had watched Eden pound out the dough over the counter with her bare hands, batch after batch with unmatched skill. After the trek to the peak, everyone delves into the food with added gusto. I would miss this food. Knowing this is my last meal in this place, I eat as many helpings as I am allowed, lingering over the third plate.

The couple arrives at the gate, and they do in fact have with them a baby, a toddler limp and fevered in his mother's arms. Eden quickly whips up a batch of thick cream from one of the goats, with a dash of gruel for thickening. The child responds right away to the bottle of homemade formula.

The others crowd around, smiling and cooing. It occurs to me that all of them, except for Alma, have lived in relative safety for most of their lives. Maybe this eagerness towards laughter is something that comes from a life of safety, life before the Fall. I stand at the door silently watching. The man and woman sit across from Eden with their hands clasped together, their faces aglow with gratitude.

"Come over and see," Alma beckons me.

"I don't think so," I reply placing my hand on my stomach. "I think I'm going to lie down. Not feeling terribly well."

"Okay then. See you tomorrow." Her gaze lingers, but I duck out and return to my room.

Finally, nightfall arrives. Going through the motions of bedtime, I kick off my shoes and lie down, climbing under the blanket. My eyes remain open and I lay still, listening to the sounds of nightfall. Waiting. Carefully waiting.

When all grows dark and quiet, I slip out of bed, placing one foot down at a time, moving with utmost stealth. I pick up my shoes, stashing them into my backpack, and slip barefooted down the hallway towards the living room. All is quiet and I think everyone is asleep. Apparently, I am mistaken.

Eden moves around the kitchen, and I stand at the edge of the door, as still as a statue. I could be out in seconds, but I am trapped. If I go across she would see me as clear as day. If I can get out undetected, I will have time to get to the warehouse and find my crossbow.

"You might as well come in," Eden calls. "I know you're snooping around out there."

I swallow hard before stepping around the corner and into the light of the kitchen. Eden takes a teapot from the stove and pours into the two mugs sitting on the table. She motions for me to sit and I do so, perched forward to avoid my backpack.

"I take it you heard what I said, today, eh?" she begins, scooting the mug towards me.

Her words and calm demeanor strike a feeling of discomfort more than I have felt in a long time. All I can do is nod.

"I suppose it would be only fair to let you have a say in what happens next." She reaches into the folds of her skirts and pulls out the photograph placing it on the table between us. "That's you, right?"

I nod again.

"My boy told me a little bit about what happened out there today. I know he said he was beholden to you not to, but there is a bigger picture here, Ash. He said he felt right sorry to do it, but he had to tell me what he saw."

She picks up the photograph. The image of the little girl from so long ago makes me feel more frightened than I had in a long while.

"Do you know what this means?" Eden says.

"No," I reply, my voice small and trembling.

"This building is where it began," she continues. "For a little while, we still had television, and the news said there was a laboratory. Government probably, not that it matters now. But this building, the lobby there, the curve of the table in the back there, that's where it all began."

"Where what all began?" I lean forward to get a better look at the picture.

"They did experiments there. Strange, unspeakable experiments."

"What kind of experiments?"

"Hard to say." She eyes me evenly. "I thought maybe you might know since it's a might evident you spent some time there."

A flush of embarrassment and anger washes over me. I don't like what she is saying and I especially don't like the way she is holding the photograph as if her fingerprints left behind are a testament to her judgment.

"But then something went wrong. No one knows exactly what. Do you know, Ash?" Eden keeps her eyes on mine as if attempting to see behind them and into my mind. I do not turn away.

The photograph trembles between her fingers, extended out as she peers over the edge at me. I take a deep breath, adjusting my backpack, and bracing myself for what will come next. Without any forecast, I pluck the photograph from her hand, lunge from the chair, and bolt for the door. With surprising quickness, she leaps after me, fingers clamping down on my arm.

"Hey!" she calls just as I twist out of her hold, darting

down the porch stairs.

My bare feet against the ground do not hinder my speed in any way. Tucking the photo into my shirt, I dash across the expanse of meadow, heading straight for the forest's edge. I head for the spot close to the spring, where the ground dips just enough underneath the fence. I might suffer a few scrapes, but it is the only way out.

"Abraham!" Eden shrieks, her voice edged in something close to panic. "Abraham! She's getting away!"

I continue forward, the needles of the forest floor sticking to my bare feet. I run, not knowing what would happen if they caught me. By the time I make it to the fence, someone is crashing through the branches a good way behind me.

After finding the gate and making it through the inner layer, I crouch down, peering back. I don't see them, but in the darkness of the forest it is no guarantee of safety. Shoving my backpack through the hole, I plaster myself to the muddy ground and elbow-crawl underneath, ignoring the metal barbs grasping at my clothing. I push my way through, keeping my face above the mud and water.

Once through I stumble to my feet, grab my backpack and run, seeking to put some distance between myself and them. The edge of the forest is not that far ahead and beyond that is the road. Losing such a safe haven brings me a pang of regret. I make it as far as the road before I stop running. My lungs burn and my feet are bleeding. Once I lose my pursuers, I will need to tend to them.

Their voices fade behind me and I move quickly down the road, confident they will not catch up with me. The only other sound is the pounding of my own heartbeat, echoing through my head. Maybe this is why I do not hear the silent black car sliding up the road, until it appears out of the night next to me. Before I can react, the door opens. Arms grab me around the waist, yanking me inside without coming to a complete stop.

I cry out, but a cloth clamps down on my face, drenched in some kind of strong chemical burning my throat. My body twists and struggles, but already weakness is taking over my limbs, preventing me from catching a glimpse of my captors. My arms are pinned to my side, legs and feet flailing against the darkened windows.

Everything goes black.

Nine

Incessant beeping cuts through the darkness pulling me back to consciousness. Underneath a thin paper gown, I realize my body is naked, and my skin smells lightly of soap. I try to move, struggling to open my eyes.

Blinking against the whiteness of the light in the small room, I raise my arm to cover my eyes, only to find a tubing device dripping a clear liquid into my body. The sheets are cool against my bare legs. My hair is clean. The feel of it is completely different than I am used to, smooth and sliding between my fingers. I sit up, trying to orient myself to my surroundings. All I see at first is walls, so beige they are nearly white. My head is swarming with bees.

"Where am I?" I say out loud, hoping the sound of my own voice will help to ground me, still unconvinced that this is not a dream. My voice sounds dry and raspy and I don't expect anyone to respond.

"Hello, Ashley." A woman's voice crackles from a loudspeaker, a wooden box nailed to the wall above the door opposite me.

"Hello? Who's there?" I say feeling my skin crawl.

"You are in a safe place, Ashley," the woman says. Her voice is soothing, as if she is smiling at the other end of... where ever she is. "We have to keep you quarantined for a few more days and then you will be able to come out. You will no longer be in any danger."

"What kind of danger would I be in?" I ask as I swing my

legs over the side.

"Don't worry about that right now," she continues. "I am so sorry it has to be this way, Ashley. It must be so disorienting for you."

I sit up and examine the port in my arm. The tubing enters at the crook of my elbow and the surrounding skin feels cold to the touch. A thick, clear tape covers the contraption, but I can still bend my arm as needed.

"Right." I stand and roll the I.V. across the room, trailing my fingers along the drab, beige walls. The door is locked, solid against my ministrations against the silver handle. I find no discernible windows anywhere in the room. "Where are you?"

"We are in the same building, just in another location."

"We?" I ask. "Who is 'we?' Who else is with you?"

"Our location has determined a three-day quarantine. In the meantime, food will be sent to you through the dumbwaiter there behind you."

I turn, dragging the I.V. stand along with me. Her instructions lead me to a portal in the wall. It appears to be a standard dumbwaiter with a metal sliding door painted the same drab beige as the walls. I peer once more at the clear liquid dripping into my body.

"Saline. Nothing more," she says. "It is a means to rehydrate you and bring you back to full health. You have been through quite an adventure these last few years."

"Where are my things?"

"We had no choice but to burn the clothing, but don't worry. We kept your personal items. They will be returned to you upon your completion of the quarantine."

I couldn't help but think about the photograph. "What do I call you?" I say. "What's your name?"

She pauses for a long while until I think she is gone. When she speaks again I sense a hesitation in her voice. "For now, you may call me Maggie."

"I am beginning to feel ridiculous talking to thin air like this."

"Ashley, I can't tell you how thrilled we are to have found you. Everything will be understood in due time, but you need to rest. You have a lot ahead of you."

"What do I have ahead of me?" I ask as I run my hands along the surface of the dumbwaiter. Finding no weak points, I slam my hands against the surface, creating a loud dissonant sound echoing through the room. The stinging in my fingers and palms wakes me up. It feels good. I do it again, hoping to feel the painted metal move in one direction or another. But there is not so much as a shudder.

"Go and lay down Ashley," she croons.

I feel a shift in the air of the room and all thoughts of escape leave my mind. My vision begins to fade. I form a fist and make contact once more with the metal door. The pain revives me again but only for a moment. Something filters through the vents against the far wall and all I can think of is the bed. My feet are sluggish but I manage to drag the silver pole back to the bed, enticing and comfortable, not stopping until I am horizontal, pulling the thin sheet over my body.

The lights are dim when I open my eyes. With no way to know how long I have been asleep, I shift slightly taking account of how my body feels. They drugged me. I know that much. So, wherever they are in the building, they have control over the atmosphere of the room. The next thing I notice is the incredible urgent need to empty my bladder. I lower my feet to the cold floor, crossing over to the door.

Still locked.

"Um....Maggie?" I call out.

A moment passes.

"Hello?" I say.

"Yes, Ashley," someone replies, but her voice is not Maggie's. She sounds young. Not much older than myself perhaps.

"Um... I wondered if there was someplace I could pee."

"There is a restroom behind the bed for your privacy where you can void."

Void, I think. *What. The. Hell.*

The bathroom is smaller than the one at Eden's. Once there, I can examine the port in my arm without worrying about being seen. The tape peels from the crook of my elbow with ease, but the tubing takes a bit of a tug. It stings as I remove it, but it does not bleed much. I jab a wad of toilet paper in the crook of my arm and return to the main room.

"There is a meal for you in the dumbwaiter," the woman says through the intercom. "You shouldn't have any trouble opening the door."

Sliding the door open proves to be harder than expected. Perhaps I put a dent in it after all. With one more hitch, it slides free, revealing a tray with a flat silver cover over the plate. I set the tray aside and run my fingers through and around the inside of the enclosure. This might actually work. I climb inside the dumbwaiter and pull the door closed behind me. My eyes squeeze shut for a moment in attempt to ignore the claustrophobic sensation creeping up my shoulders, as I press my back against the metal wall of the cubicle. The only light is the line from underneath the door.

The light soon disappears as the lift begins to move, creating a flip-flop sensation in my stomach. I weigh more than a tray of food, but this thing seems solid enough. A few seconds pass by. For a moment I wonder if I will be somehow trapped in here forever, locked in this tiny coffin traveling upwards to a level out of reach, as cold panic clutches at my throat.

The dumbwaiter comes to a stop. The door opens.

My eyes take a moment to adjust, but I see a hand extended to help me climb out. I take the hand, carefully exiting the dumbwaiter and adjusting the gown around my chilled body as the panic drains away. Three of them, white coats and curious smiles, are watching me. Behind them, I see a wall of screens flickering pictures of the room I had just escaped.

Another woman enters through the open door to the left, catching her breath as if she had just been running. When my eyes focus on her, I realize who she is. The room grows still as reality sinks in. Every eye in the room watches my reaction.

Her hair has grayed at the edges of her face, but I know her. The woman who held my hand as a small child traveling down the elevator. The woman who encouraged me to smile as the photographer snapped the photo all those years ago. Maggie.

Margaret Donovan. She straightens the collar of the white lab coat.

"Congratulations, Ashley," she says with a smile. "You just passed your first test."

Ten

Her eyes glow and her smile widens as she speaks. In an instant, I am crushed in her embrace as she clasps her arms around my shoulders. Dr. Margaret Donovan, the woman who raised me and of whom I have little memory. I stiffen at the contact and step back as soon as she lets go. My instinct is to put as much space as possible between the two of us, and I cannot keep from crossing my arms over the thin paper gown. The other scientists watch on with eyes darting back and forth between us.

"What test?" I say in what I can only hope is an unwavering voice.

The dull beige room from which I have just escaped is visible at various angles on each screen jutting from the observation deck. I scratch at the crook of my arm where I had removed the I.V. It itches terribly. Someone flips a switch and the lights go dim in the room below.

"We wanted to see how resilient you are to a foreign environment, to start with, but you showed remarkable skill and determination in finding the means of escape."

Her words make little sense to me. "To what?" I stammer.

"Oh, Ashley." She grasps my shoulders, her eyes nearly brimming. "You have no idea how remarkable you are. Do you?"

I do not answer.

"Come with me. I'll show you to your room and you can get into some proper clothing."

She takes me by the hand and leads me out of the room.

Despite my distrust of this woman, I know I need to find out what this place is. The sooner I can get my bearings, the quicker I can find a way out.

The hallway has shiny white walls and beige trim, calm and sterile. Imagining the lights gone and paper cluttering the floor, it is identical to the abandoned laboratory where I had found the photograph.

"Where are you taking me?" I ask.

"To your room."

We arrive at a large double door leading to another hall with a markedly different atmosphere. The floor is carpeted with ornate designs, golden flowers against a maroon background. Gilded trim lines the taupe colored walls. We pass several doors built from rich red wood, gleaming and decadent. My bare feet sink into the thick carpet, and it reminds me of the thick mossy ground in the midst of the forests.

"This is going to be your home for a little while," she says as we turn the corner.

"Is it?" I reply.

"Yes," she says with a laugh. "I understand this must be so disorienting for you, but I can assure you we want nothing but for you to feel at home here. After all, you *are* home."

We reach the door at the end of the hall and come to a stop.

"Go on," she says with that incessant smile. "Open it."

I take a breath and turn the gold handle.

The furniture is bright shades of lavender, purple, and pink shades foreign to the vine-covered cityscapes to which I had grown accustomed. The space is filled with an enormous bed piled with pillows and ruffles, a bookshelf, and posters of smiling movie stars adorning the walls. What strikes me immediately is that this room is identical to the one in which I lived as a child before the Fall.

I step inside, momentarily shocked by the wave of Deja Vu. The nostalgia of the surroundings threatens my emotions, but I push them aside with the realization that this is exactly the reaction she is most likely hoping for. Connection. Longing for home.

She proceeds to flutter around the room, straightening here and there, smoothing out the bed covers. "There are towels in the bathroom, so you can get cleaned up. If you need anything, just press this button here." She pauses at the door. "You may call me Dr. Donovan or Maggie if that isn't too informal. There was a time when you called me 'Mother,' but your memory has been compromised. I understand if you are not comfortable with that just yet."

"There is one thing," I say.

"Yes, of course."

"My backpack?"

She trots across the room to a closet door the same sickly pink shade as the wall, opening it to reveal a small room lined with clothing. She reaches in and pulls out my backpack, holding it out to me. Despite my desire to remain stoic, I grab it from her, clinging to the one familiar thing in the whole compound.

"Ashley," she says in her simpering tone. "You have been through so much, I know. Why don't you get settled here? Pick out something to wear. Take your time. I'll come back in a couple of hours to show you around and introduce you to the others." She walks towards the door to exit, pausing at the frame and turning back towards me. "You are not a prisoner here. Please don't think that, Ashley."

For a moment, her face reveals a glimpse of genuine friendliness and I wonder if I am responding too harsh towards her.

"Is there anything else I can do for you at this time?" she says.

"Just one," I reply. "My name is Ash."

"Ash. Of course," she replies with a thin pressed smile before she pulls the door closed behind her, leaving me alone.

The first thing I do is open the backpack and examine the contents. Everything is there, even the photograph. Myself as a child, standing hand-in-hand alongside a younger version of the same woman who just left. Why I feel a strange affection for the woman in the picture, but a cold disdain for the same woman in person is difficult for me to understand. Perhaps there is some memory yet to be unlocked which holds the answer.

I step to the closet. Mesmerized, I run my fingers over the selection of clothing. On one side hangs several pairs of pants leading to a collection of brightly colored dresses. I pass over them thinking them impractical. Out there, it had not been difficult to gather selections of clothing from the abandoned stores. I always stocked up on tee shirts when I had the chance.

I choose a pair of jeans and a fitted black cotton tee shirt, something in which I could easily move if needed. The shoes have rubber soles with thick padding around the foot, made for running which may come in handy. Next, I examine the room, my eyes darting around the corners, suspecting they may be watching me, even here.

Dr. Donovan arrives a few moments after I press the button and we return back the way we came, towards the laboratory. Just at the end of the hall, she stops and presses a panel on the wall. I realize then that there is a set of doors inset into the paneling which opens to a staircase and sliding doors leading to an elevator.

"Here we are," she says.

The doors open and we step inside, closed in and surrounded by reflective walls on all sides. I am overcome with a wave of Deja Vu when she smiles at me just as she had when I was a child.

"Is everything alright?" She draws together her eyebrows.

"Yes, I'm fine," Even though my stomach flips at the movement of the elevator, leaving me disoriented. I place my hand on the bar along the elevator wall until the unit comes to a stop. The door opens and we step into an open courtyard and glorious fresh air.

"This way." She gestures down a paved footpath.

People come and go all around us, laughing and smiling. Again, I notice the lack of urgency I witnessed in the members of Eden's farm. These people are the same. Living in assumed safety changes people's demeanor.

The sun pierces my vision as we move towards a patio extended from a squat brick building in the center of the courtyard. Through the expansive open window, I see people scurrying and sounds of metal clanking together. We approach one of the metal grid tables and sit down. She motions to a girl with deep red hair, close to my age, darting to and from the surrounding tables.

"Rose, can you bring us a tray please?"

"Right away," she replies, casting me nothing more than a quick glance before disappearing into the building. Around us, the others sit and eat with casual, slow comfort, sitting up straight, chatty and relaxed. It makes no sense.

"How are you feeling?" Maggie asks, pulling my attention back to her.

"Oh, I'm fine," I insist. "Maybe a bit disoriented, but I'm okay. Really."

"The food will help. I am sure."

Within another few minutes, the young woman named Rose returns, balancing an oval tray containing two plates of food. The one she sets down in front of me, contains a stacked sandwich made of puffy bread, a large slab of grilled, ground meat. Next to it, lies a pile of golden, glistening sticks which smell of salt and earth. Maggie's plate contains the same food. I watch her to see what she does. She picks up a golden stick and takes a bite off the end, and I do my best to mimic her movements to avoid drawing attention to myself.

The food is delicious and unlike anything I have tasted before. It does much to make me feel better, but I know I have to keep my composure. I need them to trust me. More importantly, I need them to think I trust them.

"Okay," I say pushing away my now empty plate. "Are you ready to tell me what this is all about?"

"I'm sorry," she says clasping her hands before her. "This all must seem so strange to you. I apologize for all the theatrics. It is all just so exciting. I can't wait to show you everything. Would you like to have a tour?"

“That would be wonderful,” I reply.

I stand and follow her, taking in the details of the compound as we move along. The expanse of the courtyard is large enough that I cannot see the far end except that it is surrounded by buildings. A metal staircase leads up the side of a brick building. There are no apparent exits between the buildings, each connecting to the other forming an expansive wall around the circumference, not one of them is less than three stories tall. We walk along the spider web of paths stretched across the grassy area, accessorized by a square-edged shrubbery.

“This place was built long before the Fall,” she begins. “Those of us left, consider it our duty to uphold the ideals of the human race, what is left of us. And we are proud to do so. There are seven of these compounds across the country. One of which you grew up in, as you may have guessed. Each compound is completely secure. Nothing can get inside the perimeter.”

“But why?” I ask, pausing as we approach the sidewalk running in front of the buildings. “Why did they build this place if nothing had happened yet? How did they know what was coming?”

She considers her words, continuing slowly as if reciting a memorized passage. “There had been isolated incidents. Whatever this was, had come to the attention of certain powerful parties long before reaching the public's knowledge. They called it the Z plague. At first as a bit of a joke, but once it became apparent what the potential was, no resource was spared in building these places. They already knew it was only a matter of time before something went wrong...”

"Went wrong...?" Something sparks in my mind, reaching for a puzzle piece just out of reach.

"Sadly, yes." She gestures towards a towering building with two spires jutting towards the pale sky. "This is the school building where the others take their lessons. You'll be joining them after we complete all your tests. We want you to be comfortable and get acclimated as soon as possible."

"Tell me more about the Fall. How did they know what would happen?"

"Oh, they didn't specifically know this would happen," she continues as we meander on down the path. "But they always knew it would be something. Nuclear war, biological warfare... There was always some apocalypse or another being kept at bay. Honestly, there were many surprised it didn't come sooner."

We have circled around the length of the courtyard, returning back to the elevator entrance at the base of the building.

"This building is the main laboratory, some of which you have already seen. This is the place where they are trying to recreate the molecular reaction which caused the plague in the first place. Once they do, it could lead us to a more efficient antidote. The living quarters are here as well, for many of the scientists and their families."

"There is something I don't understand," I say. "What does any of this have to do with me? Why did I grow up the way I did, and why don't I remember any of it?"

She nods, pressing her lips together and clasping her hands behind her back. "Come with me," she says. We step once more into the coffin-like elevator which lifts us without ceremony to the third floor.

"Once the government realized this virus had the potential to erupt into epidemic proportions, work began immediately to find a vaccine. Several experiments took place in attempt to create antibodies within an existing bloodline. Keep in mind, this happened long before the actual Fall."

Up ahead, a floor to ceiling picture window spills a cheerful yellow light onto the linoleum floor of the hallway. As we approach, I see smiling, cartoon animal faces sticking to the glass overlooking a room filled with couches on one side and cribs lining the wall around one corner of the room. A gentle-faced woman stands bouncing one of the babies against her hip, a fat and happy child gnawing on a chubby fist.

Behind her a young man straightens up, his back to us, having just laid down one of the children in a crib. I guess his age at about two years older than me. He brushes away a stray lock of auburn hair and immediately I see the resemblance to the girl who had brought us our food earlier. He glances our way, giving a quick wave.

"There was one successful strain of antibodies found," Maggie continues. "They have been trying to replicate the circumstances ever since. These children here are the product of that experiment. Oh, don't worry! They are healthy in every way. Born just as any of us have been. But after that first case, success has evaded us."

I cross my arms in front of me, unable to pinpoint the source of my discomfort.

"Would you like to go inside?"

"Inside?" I reply. "I don't... I mean, I've never..."

"Come on," she pushes open the door inviting me inside. "The nursery is one of the areas we are most proud of. If we cannot pinpoint the antidote, at least we have a good start on rebuilding a healthy population, right?"

"I suppose so," I mutter as I step through the door. The room is filled with babbles and occasional fussy cries. Two infants sit on the carpet sharing a wooden beaded wire toy. The woman passes off the child to the young man and steps towards me.

"I'm Eva," she says with a wide smile and an outstretched hand. "It's nice to meet you. This is my son, Thorn. Rose tells me she made your acquaintance at lunch today."

"Oh?" I feel a bit overwhelmed by the enthusiasm with which everyone speaks in this place. My mind drifts momentarily to Rachel and Marcus, seeing before me a life denied to both of them.

"Ah, speaking of which." Eva continues, turning back towards me. "Why don't you come have dinner with us tonight? We can give you an insider's perspective on this place. I'll send Rose to come pick you up." She glances towards Maggie. "If that is alright with you, that is."

Maggie shrugs. "Well, I don't see why not. The remainder of the tests do not begin until tomorrow. I think it might be good for you to get to know some of the others close to your age, Ash."

"Um... sure, okay," I reply.

Eva and Maggie exchange a few more words. Thorn watches me with intense curiosity, eyes unwavering until, just as sudden he turns his attention to one of the toddlers on the carpet in the middle of the room, rolling a red rubber ball to the delighted, squealing child.

"The nursery used to be much larger," Maggie says after we exit the room. "But as you can imagine, it is difficult as the children age up. Do you have any questions at this point?"

"Yes. Why do I have to go through these tests? Is it because I lived out there?"

She pauses just at the elevator, her eyes wide. "Oh, Ash. You still don't see it, do you?"

"See what?"

"That first case, the successful one in which we were able to localize the antibodies... Ash, that child was you."

I do nothing to soften the glare I aim at her.

"The experiments indicated an antibody within your blood which could be drawn out to perfect the vaccine before it became too late. I adopted you right away, of course, raised you as my own. They called you Baby A when you first arrived at the facilities. It was I who named you Ashley. The name suited you. "

The elevator doors open. Without a word, I step inside.

"We kept you in the laboratory," she continues as she follows me in. "Oh, I know it sounds dreadful, but knowing what we did, we felt we had no choice. It was not nearly as clinical as it sounds. You had a nursery and around the clock care. As you grew, we made sure your every need was met. There was a playground, you might remember."

"A playground," I repeat the word trying to recall the meaning.

"When the Fall happened it came on faster than we had

anticipated, even in our worst case scenarios. We did not have time to trigger the quarantine protocol fast enough. It's a shame really. We were right on the verge..."

She stops and a distant gaze drifts across her face.

"But as I said," she waves her hands, brushing aside whatever memory had made her pause, "we have all the time in the world now. The room we have for you is an exact replica. We did our best to replicate it, hoping it might trigger your memories. The clothes are different of course. Somehow during your absence, you have managed to turn into a young lady."

The door slides open and we step out onto an open air patio. Concrete leading to a walled edge. I can see by the placement of the other buildings that we are on the top of the wall surrounding the compound. I follow her to the edge and see a birds-eye view of the courtyard below. At this height, the wind whistles around us, pulling my hair every which way around my head. I clutch my arms across my chest against the chill.

"When you were evacuated," she continues. "The memory chip in your brain was triggered to erase any evidence of your upbringing."

"Memory chip..." I say. "That's why I can't remember."

"Yes. Implanted when you were still an infant. I'm so sorry it had to come to that. Powerful people knew of your potential. It would have been dangerous for you to fall into the wrong hands."

"More dangerous than living in a world of flesh-eating monsters?" I say, between chattering teeth.

"I think we both know that would not present much of a danger to you. Isn't that right?"

She crosses over to the other side of the wall. I follow her over, seeing the outside world once more, the world from which I came. In the distance, I spot a metal chain fence marking yet another layer of security. The space in between is filled with zombies, roaming and mindless, creating an unbreakable barrier surrounding the outer wall of the compound. Whatever veneer of politeness between us since I awoke in that blinding room begins to drift away into the distant, white sky.

"Ashley," she says. "I raised you. I know you don't remember, but you are like a daughter to me. I want, perhaps more than anyone here, for the series of tests to be as easy as possible for you."

I place my hands on the grainy concrete edge of the wall.

"But," she hesitates, glancing down at the expanse of gnarling monsters below us. At first, I think she is expressing regret but when she returns her gaze to me, what I see in her eyes sends chills down my spine. "If we have to, we can do this the hard way. Do you understand?"

"I understand." I keep my expression frozen as I reply. It is clear I need to play along for now.

The doors slide open and I step out of the elevator into the courtyard. She parted ways with me on the third floor, returning to the laboratory and insisting that I go and explore the compound. The solitude feels good, especially after the exchange on the wall. I find myself missing the outside, despite its unpredictable dangers.

I stroll along the path circling the edge of the patio. Rose is standing at a table close to me, stacking the plates and moving the utensils to the top of the pile. As she reaches across the table, her hand pauses. She does not look my way, but I know without any doubt that what she does next is for my benefit. Her hand pauses at the edge of the plates, her index and middle fingers forming a V shape, just for a moment before she relaxes her hand and picks up the stack of plates. The signal, ever so brief, flashes in my mind, waking a long dormant memory.

Something bad had happened. Everyone was panicking. Running, screaming. The young woman scientist who had always been nice to me, clutched my arm just above my elbow, pulling me along at a steady pace down the hall.

"Get her over the mountains," she said. "She'll be safe there."

"Which way?"

"East. Get her to the coast and she'll be safe."

The tall, brown-skinned man grabbed me from her and rushed me to the car. On some level, I knew what was happening as he ushered me into the vehicle. In a way I did not yet understand, this was about me. All of it.

The wheels skidded out of the parking lot of the building, chaos erupting all around us. His fingers flashed the 'V' to the woman in the window, the one who had grabbed me from my room, the one who had saved me. She stood at the window peering down at us. Lost forever, because the containment border had already been closed behind us.

I twisted my head around, trying to catch a glimpse as we sped away from my home. The last thing I saw was the woman standing there, one palm at the window, tears streaming down her face. Her other hand held up as a symbol of rebellion, her fingers signaled the V back to him.

Not even a moment has passed. Our eyes meet for another second. Her face remains expressionless. She turns back to her work, picking up the dishes and disappearing back inside. For a moment, I think I have imagined it all. I have no idea what the V symbolizes, but the rush of memory allows me a newfound clarity. There is more going on here than I realize. Much more.

Eleven

I find no weaknesses in the walls of my room. Other than the door and the window overlooking the courtyard, there are no seams anywhere. I examine the window pane, a plexiglass of some kind, determined by the way it subtly springs back from my fingertips when I apply pressure. Unbreakable. This is a gilded cage, and I am its prisoner. I sit down at the edge of the bed and consider my next move.

At my window, the sun crosses the sky, appearing like a distant burnished coin hanging against a white canvas. The cloying décor of the room makes me feel uncomfortable. The surroundings are so unnatural here. At least at Eden's farm, most of my time was spent outside. The 'V' must be a code of some kind. I need to find out more.

The grumbling in my stomach reminds me that I need to eat again soon. Rose should be by to pick me up at some point. The lack of urgency at finding a meal, of not having to scavenge and hunt for food, still feels strange to me. I could just walk down to the courtyard and someone would bring me food. It feels like cheating.

The sharp squawk of the buzzer breaks my reverie.

"Hi," the red-headed girl says with a wide smile when I open the door. "I hope you're hungry. Mom's made fettuccine and meatballs. We haven't officially met, I guess. My name is Rose."

She juts her hand out towards me, and I tentatively clasp her fingers with my own.

"Sorry, I tend to talk a lot when I'm nervous. Come on. We

can take the stairs. Most of us do. No one wants to be stuck in the elevators when the power goes out. It doesn't happen very often, but when it does, it's kind of a bitch. The solar power is touch-and-go depending on the time of year."

She continues speaking as we head down the hallway. We step through to the stairs and head up. With some bit of surprise, I find myself drawn to her, as if we could have been friends in another lifetime.

"We live on the fifth level," she continues. "Ashley, right?"

"Ash. I feel more comfortable if you call me Ash."

Their apartment exudes a homey vibrancy, so different from the abandoned shells I was used to on the outside. Eva moves in and out of the kitchen, where inviting smells waft towards us. Off the main room is a man sitting at a desk, pouring over a collection of papers. He pushes up the thick-rimmed glasses perched on his nose, squinting from the documents up to the blue glowing screen at the corner of his desk.

"Hi, Dad," Rose chirps.

"Hello," he mumbles, eyes scanning back and forth across his documents.

Eva brings a bowl to the center of the table, filled with a food I have never seen before. Some kind of pasta with a thick red sauce. Tiny orbs of meat line the edges of the bowl. It smells divine. Rose's father appears and takes his seat, portioning out a serving onto his plate.

"This must be quite a change for you, Ash," Eva says taking the seat across from me. "Rose, do you mind to call your brother and let him know dinner is ready?"

“Thorn!” Rose calls down the hall loud enough to make me jump. He appears a moment later, skulking into the room and giving me a wary glance as he takes his seat at the table.

“It is a bit of an adjustment,” I reply to Eva.

“Well, it is certainly a pleasure to finally meet you. The kids learned about you in school, you know. Your childhood is part of the curriculum.”

Some of the words she uses don't have a meaning, but I stay silent.

“You know,” Rose says, leaning in next to me. “You're practically a celebrity around here. Everyone wants to know about you. The real you anyway.”

“What's a celebrity?”

“Wow. You really are just like they say...” Rose's father leans forward, joining the conversation for the first time. “Remarkable!”

“And what do they say?” I reply, feeling the same annoyance as when my crossbow jams.

“That you are like a wild animal,” he continues.

Out of the corner of my eye, Thorn rolls his eyes and shakes his head.

“Oh, I don't mean that in a bad way,” he sputters. “Not at all! It's just that, I mean... we've never met anyone from the outside before. Much less...”

“You'll have to forgive our dad,” Thorn says in an even tone. “He can't seem to shut down his scientist's brain over dinner. Everything is a specimen to him. Something to be studied and poked at. Isn't that right, Dad?”

"Boys," Eva interjects. "Let's not start. We have a guest this evening. Let's behave ourselves. Shall we?"

"You know what?" Rose says, the brightness in her voice immediately lightens the atmosphere. "A bunch of us are meeting at the rec room tonight after dinner, around eight o'clock. You should come. Everyone is just *dying* to meet you."

Dying to meet me? I wonder. This place is a mystery, but I am comforted by the presence of this family. It is not difficult to understand, as I observe the banter between them all, that the jabs are meant in a friendly way. Their father, I find out, is one of the scientists and works in the lab with Dr. Donovan. I eat the rest of my food, enjoying once more the foreign feeling of not having to hunt for it.

"I hate to ask this," I say quietly to Rose as the adults are cleaning up the table after. "But what does 'eight o'clock' mean?"

Her eyes widen for a moment before she smiles and begins her explanation. "The power grid goes down at ten. Most of the kids like to meet up at the end of the day, just to chill for a few hours before curfew."

I have no idea what she means. Now and then a phrase will spark a moment of recognition, an echo of familiarity from a long time ago. But despite these fleeting hints of clarity, I cannot find a way to place the words in context in my mind. It makes me feel disconnected from everyone around me.

"Why don't you kids go on over," Eva says with a smile. "I'll come and pick you up in time for curfew."

Rose nods and grabs my hand. "You ready to learn how to play ping pong?"

"Um...sure."

"Thorn, are you coming?"

"Yeah, I'll come."

We move quickly down the hallway with Thorn following along behind us. The memory of the signal, the 'V' shaped fingers, continues to bug me. Perhaps it means something different here than it had from my childhood. Perhaps I had imagined the whole thing. Since this afternoon, I had not seen anyone using the sign again.

We arrive at the rec room. The kids gathered, range in age from maybe ten to the late teens, close to Rose's age. Games are scattered everywhere. Colorful boxes and books line the shelves. In one corner a couch and large plush seats surround a small table. There are about twenty kids in all, more people than I have ever seen in my life. Not counting the zombies of course.

When we enter the broad room, I sense a shift in everyone's attention. A few eyes dart my way and the lively conversation drops into a subtle murmur. Rose gives me an encouraging smile and takes me over to one of the game tables.

"You have to understand," she says in a quiet voice so only I can hear. "Everyone here has grown up on the inside. You are the only one who knows what it's like out there."

"I guess that's true."

Rose picks up a paddle and gestures to the other one at my end of the table.

I pick it up, watching her to see what happens next. She picks up the tiny white ball and volleys it towards me, creating a small *pock* sound as it hits the table. On instinct, I block it with my paddle, sending it back towards her. She hits back. We go back and forth like this for a while. Out of the corner of my eye, I notice everyone watching us, one at at time putting down what they are doing and making their way towards us.

"She's good," someone whispers.

"Of course she is," someone else responds. "Think about it."

"But Rose is the best player on the compound."

"Shh! Let's see what happens."

Finally, a hush falls over them as the volleying turns into an intensity between the two of us. Rose leans in, a playful smile dancing on her lips. An emotion sparks within me, a feeling of happiness and warmth underneath my heart. An experience which would be fleeting in my usual life. The volleys speed up. I can see the beading of sweat breaking out across Rose's forehead.

The ball hits the edge of the table just inside the white line, flying wild. I leap for it with everything I have and only just knock it back. The ball sails past Rose, who shrieks as is whooshes past the edge of her paddle. Those watching us break into applause as Rose gasps, hands on her knees and beaming a broad smile.

"That was...fun," I say.

"Oh, so she does know about fun," Rose says.

"What is it like out there?" a young girl asks from the back of the gathered group. I turn to answer her and realize that every eye is on me, waiting for an answer. I consider what Rose said, that none of them have any idea what the outside is like. I think about the view from the top of the wall. They must have seen it. I sit down on the couch as the others gather around me.

"Have any of you been out there?" I begin.

"No. No one," the girl replies. "We've heard stories of course, but..."

"There aren't as many as there used to be," I say. "It isn't difficult to get around. They are easy to avoid, and they don't move very quickly."

"What's the most dangerous thing about being out there?" an older boy asks.

"When they gather up in a horde," I reply without hesitation. "If they outnumber you, it could mean trouble. If you can get up a tree or into a shelter, you might have a chance. But the real danger is the people. That kind of world, it messes with people. Everyone is fighting for survival."

"Have you ever been over the mountains?" Thorn asks. He is leaning against the ping pong table with his arms crossed, standing further back, separate from the others. At first, I don't quite know what he means.

"No, I never have."

He exchanges a glance with Rose. I almost miss it. Nothing more than a flick of his gaze.

"I have some questions for all of you," I say. "I've been told that my childhood is something you have learned about. Is this true?"

"It is," the younger girl says. "Everyone finds out about Baby A around the third grade. The first of your kind. They haven't been able to replicate another one like you."

"Replicate?" I say. "What do you mean by that?"

"I think Ash has been through enough," Rose says with sudden intensity. "Besides it's almost curfew. We should let her go and get some rest. We can ask more questions tomorrow when we have time."

"Incoming!" Thorn stands up, glancing towards the door. A few at the outskirts of the circle head to various game tables, picking up as if they had been playing the whole time. Others flip open their books and take on a pose of lounging against the padded arms of the couch.

"Now's your cue," Rose whispers, giving me a nudge.

Just as the door swings open, I pose my hands in front of me while the remainder of the group affects expressions of rapt wonder.

"And I shot it right in the eye!" I declare.

The audience plays their part, gasping and applauding with impressed acceptance.

"Hey, Mom!" Rose chirps as Eva enters the room.

"Time for curfew," she replies.

"What happens at curfew?" I ask.

"The energy is shut down. We conserve what we can to build up the solar power. You will learn about that once you start school. I'll walk you back and I can tell you more about it. Rose, Thorn, I'll meet you two back at the apartment."

I glance at Rose. She nods. I scan the room before I step through the door. Thorn watches me from the far side of the room with a hesitant gaze. I turn away and head down the hallway, Eva pacing right behind me.

"Are you finding your way around the compound okay?"

she asks.

"I think so." Being around her makes me feel comfortable, at ease.

"It's good for you to be making friends. I can't imagine what it must have been like for you out there all by yourself."

"I got by."

She laughs, a light and delicate sound. "I'm sure you did. What I mean is, I think you have a good chance here. We think it is important you become acclimated to the life in the compound as soon as possible. To fit in."

We approach the elevator and step inside.

"Did Maggie give you the tour of the place?" Eva says.

"Yes, she did."

"By chance, did she tell you about the East hallway? The restricted part of the laboratory?"

"No, I don't think so."

"Hm..." Eva crosses her hands in front of her and stares straight ahead.

"What is the East hallway?" I ask. "Why is it restricted?"

The elevator lurches to a stop and the doors slide open. "I don't think it is my place to tell you. I am sure it will all be explained in time. I guess we'll see you in the morning."

"Okay. Thank you for dinner."

"It was my pleasure."

I step out.

"Ash," she calls almost as an afterthought.

I turn back to her, thinking perhaps there was something she had forgotten to tell me.

“Be careful,” was her only admonishment. As the doors slide shut, she raises her left arm and just at the last second, her fingers form the shape of a 'V'.

I am alone in the hallway.

The door to my room is around the corner on one end, and the entrance to the laboratory is at the other. There is no question what I should do. Part of me wonders if I would get caught if I go snooping around in there. I can always pretend that I am sleepwalking. My newness and ignorance is one advantage I can claim at least.

Turning my back towards my room, I push through the door into the darkened laboratory.

It takes a moment for my eyes to adjust to the shadows. She had said the East hallway. I can't find any indication on the walls or doors which might give me a clue where to go. My mind relaxes and reaches out into the emptiness surrounding me.

The lab is cold, all sharp corners and hidden shadows. I find the hallway over the room where they kept me. My eyes trace the location of the dumbwaiter through the wall, the room where I escaped only to come face to face with a much greater foe.

Something is there, further down in the depths of the facility.

I feel it.

Step by step, I pass by doors on either side of me, knowing many of them are locked. Mental calculations indicate there is a level below me. I come to an intersection at the end of the hall, stretching out to the left and right.

East.

I turn to the right. Whatever I feel becomes stronger and I know I am going in the right direction. Red double doors block my way. I press my hand against the plane of the door and push it open, halfway expecting an alarm to go off, alerting the others of my presence. I step through to the other side.

A dim gray light spills from a window along the wall.

Wild dread grows in my stomach. Slowing my pace, feeling the pinpricks in the back of my neck. I think about Rose and her family, never having known the horror of coming face to face with one of them. Never having to question why they rip through the flesh of others but leave me alone, moving past me like river water around an island. Everything within me tells me not to look through that window. I fight the urge to turn back and run back to my room, to accept my placement here and become part of the community.

I step up to the window, placing my palms against the glass.

There are dozens of them, milling around in the room below. At first, I do not quite understand what I am looking at. I have seen zombie clutches before, but this one is different. It takes a few seconds for me to realize they are all female. Some have long hair, tangled and rotted. Some are broad shouldered, but delicate in stature. They wander almost in a circle, ignoring each other, vacant eyes staring forward, same shuffling gate.

"No," I whisper as realization washes over me, cold panic clutching my heart.

I fall to the floor, sliding against the glass, bile dancing on my tongue. Gasping for breath, I stumble back to my feet, moving forward. I no longer care if I am found. Panic wins this time and I run through the lab, shoving open the door back into the hallway. I don't stop until I make it back to my room. Here at least, I can pretend that I am safe.

They told me I was the first.

Now I know what that means.

Every one of them, the female zombies in that room, are all heavily pregnant.

Twelve

In the following weeks, I keep to myself as much as possible, watching and waiting, tucking away pieces of information, just as I once did supplies and food in the outside world. I tell no one about my discovery in the laboratory, not even Rose. The bits of knowledge I gather slowly begin to fall into a kind of pattern, providing me an insight into the true workings of this place.

For example, I discover that everyone else is just about as fond of Dr. Donovan as I am. The tests ensue, a series of tasks which make little sense to me; running on a treadmill, wires attached to my chest and forehead. Another day, set in a room, prompted to catch little yellow balls hurled at me from a machine. The crew of white-coats, as I have come to call them, watch me put together puzzles, stack blocks, find the next shape in a pattern, and so on.

I start planning my escape almost right away. I know I need a plan. I cannot be hasty. I play the part, jumping through the hoops set before me. Sometimes I catch her watching me, Dr. Donovan, gazing at me with a wistful expression, something akin to fondness. When I see it, I wonder why, if she raised me, why my memories don't return. At the very least I should feel something akin to familiarity towards her. It feels strange that I don't feel it, and I wonder if I ever did.

"You're getting stronger," she says after I have completed some complex obstacle course. "I think you may be ready."

"Ready for what?" I ask.

"When we found you, you were half starved out there in the wild. You are finally starting to show some muscle mass. That's good."

I decline to mention that when they 'found' me I had already been eating well for a number of weeks while working on Eden's farm. But otherwise, she was right. I was getting stronger.

"Come with me," she says. "I'd like to try something."

She holds the door open for me, and I cannot help but glance towards the hallway with the restricted red doors hiding the secrets of this place. She spoke to me glancing now and then over her shoulder as she led me down the twisted passages.

"These tests have given us a good indication of what you are capable of," she says. "I know they seem a bit pedantic, but you are worth so much more than you realize."

She says this often. I refrain from rolling my eyes.

"But there is something else, Ash. Something we would have known by now if... well... if we hadn't lost you on the day of the Fall."

She opens a double door leading out onto a short balcony flush with a courtyard. The walls surround a grassy area and the sky is pale clouds overhead. Dr. Donovan presses a button which lowers the gate. She gestures me to step forward. On the far side of the courtyard is an iron gate closing off some kind of hold. I sense the creatures within the enclosure.

"What is this?" I ask.

"It's alright, Ash. No harm will come to you." She steps back, reactivating the gate and leaving me alone in the courtyard.

I hear them, just there, gnarling and scrabbling against the walls, against each other, the smell of rotted flesh emanated from the hold, but even this was not as strong as the connection, their minds, tattered scraps of what they once were, connecting with mine.

"What's happening?" I say.

"Just remember, Ash. Remember how you used to do it as a child."

The iron gates swing open, leaving nothing between me and the flesh-hungry creatures. They move forward, attracted by my presence. A persistent memory taps at the back of my mind. I have done this before. They had forced me to walk through the hallway, closed off except for the doors on either end, filled with flesh eating monsters. She, the woman who claimed I once called her Mother, had pushed me through that door.

"I'll meet you on the other side," she had whispered with a smile on her face.

Terrified, I had walked through the milling huddle, most of the zombies shuffling past me, unnoticed. For the first time, I realized they would not touch me. I made it to the other side where I collapsed in tears into Maggie's arms. She held me, stroking my hair and cooing soft words as if she herself had not been the very person who had put me in with them moments before. I could not have been older than five.

Within the courtyard, the creatures surround me shuffling back and forth, their dead eyes focused on nothing.

"Ash, I want you to make them walk to the right side of the enclosure."

"I don't understand."

"You can do it."

I take one trembling breath before I begin, an attempt at focusing my thoughts. I make the mental adjustment, feeling the energy draining out of me, leeching into them and forcing their movements towards the right of the grassy area. In slow shuffling motions, they ambulate as one group to the far right side, those leading the pack bumping mindlessly against the wall.

"Good! Wonderful, my dear," she croons.

"What's this for--?"

"Shh. There's plenty of time for questions later. Right now you need to concentrate."

Without a moment to consider her words, a squealing fat pig appears, dropped in through a small portal on the left side. The zombies take notice of the fresh meat immediately, some semblance of hunger flashing across their rotted faces. They all throttle against each other crossing towards the frightened piglet in quick sloppy steps, bypassing me like water in a stream.

I stop them immediately, feeling that familiar sensation of tumblers falling into a lock, their will bending to mine. They hover around the piglet, not quite frozen but limbs flailing helplessly unable to reach for their victim. The trembling pig presses its body against the stone wall with no means to escape.

"Good, my dear," Dr. Donovan croons from behind me. "Now, I want you to let them go. Let them get to it."

My stomach twists at the thought. "I don't want to," I say.

"Let them go, Ash. Then we can be done for the day."

I hold them back for as long as I am able. Seconds feel like an eternity, strength draining from my body. I keep them at bay until everything goes black. As my collapsing body hits the ground I hear the squeals of the dying pig. I try my best not to think about Marcus.

When I wake, hours later based on the slant of the sun, I am back in my own room, the room they provided for me. Dr. Donovan sits at the side of my bed, watching me with that same wistful expression. She sees me stir and smiles, stroking the hair off my forehead.

"There you are, my dear," she says in a soothing voice.

"I would prefer you not call me that," I say.

"Call you what?"

"'My dear'. Despite what you think, I am not your long-lost daughter. It's clear I am nothing more to you than a guinea pig."

I turn my back and pretend to be asleep once more until she finally stands and leaves the room.

Eva had taken to having me come for dinner at least once a week. It became a bit of a routine for us. Dr. Donovan had been right about one thing. The access to food and rest have strengthened my system. I felt stronger than I had in ages.

"What does it mean?" I ask Eva one night as Thorn and their father clear the table."The V, what does it mean?"

"The V?" Eva replies.

"This." I hold up the signal with my right hand. "What is it?"

The others pause, Rose returning to the dining room from the kitchen. Eva exchanges an extended glance with her husband.

"Might as well," he says. "Especially considering..."

Eva breaks his gaze and gestures me over to the living room area. "How much do you remember?" she says. "From before I mean?"

"Not much," I reply. "It comes back here and there." The shift of the mood has me on edge. Rose enters the room, drying her hands with a dishtowel and sits down in the chair across from us.

"I have a difficult question to ask you," Eva says. "If that's okay..."

"It's alright. Go on."

"Did you find the creatures in the East hallway?" She speaks with kindness behind her voice.

"Yes. I did."

"Do you understand what it means?"

I don't want to hear it, but I have to. I need her to say the words. "Tell me."

"Your mother, Ash. Your mother was Patient Zero. Do you know what that means?"

My mouth goes dry.

Eva continues."That means she was the first one... of them."

"Tell me everything. I need to know."

She takes a breath. "The official documents say no one knows how she got it, but there is some evidence that the government created the virus. That they infected her on purpose as part of a biochemical weapons test. Your mother was part of a paid volunteer program. She hid the pregnancy from them. Apparently, she needed the money."

"Oh my god," I whisper. I glance at Rose who watches me with nervous eyes.

"She had already changed over completely by the time you were born."

Tendrils of cold horror snake up my spine.

"They kept her in a containment unit. She was put down soon after you were delivered."

She falls silent, both of them watching me. All of my emotions began to float away from me, one by one and I am left feeling empty with this truth. My fingertips feel numb.

Eva continues. "At first, you seemed like an ordinary child, but as you grew up it became evident that you were different. You were stronger, smarter, somehow more than human. They started to test your abilities around the age of three. That small part of you in your DNA is something they could not isolate. That small part is what they need to replicate."

"For the antidote," I say.

"No," she replies. "They want to make more of you."

"Make...more..."

"In you, they found the perfect super soldier. They cannot understand what makes you special, but they have never been able to replicate the same outcome.."

The tone in her voice is dark, ominous. She exchanges a glance with Rose.

"Tell her," Thorn's voice interrupts from the entry way He leans against the wall, arms crossed. "Go on. Tell her the rest of it."

"This has been going on since before the Fall. They have

kept this whole process well hidden. It did not take long before we realized what was going on. That it wouldn't stop. And that they have the gall to call it scientific research.

"There was a small faction of us who started an underground rebellion within their circles. We had to be careful though. The organization was quite powerful. That's what this means." She extends her fingers into the shape of a V. "It was one of our codes to help identify ourselves to each other. At least, that's how it started. Over time, it became a rallying symbol, a sign of encouragement to each other."

"What was the goal, of the faction I mean?"

"Several goals," Eva continues. "On the one hand, you had been a prisoner for your whole life. Dr. Donovan raised you as well as she could, giving you her name and a place to live. But the only life you ever knew was that of a lab rat really. For starters, we wanted to get you out, find a way for you to have a normal life."

"But then the Fall happened," I say, "and it was too late."

"That's exactly right."

"Mom," Thorn says, still hovering at the doorway. "I think we should tell her... about the plan."

"I think so too," Eva says. "Maggie continues to feed everyone the idea that the outside is crawling with zombies, that the only safe place is to stay within these walls."

"Yes," I say. "But it's not true anymore. It's not like it's used to be."

"That's what we've suspected. There are many of us in the community who want to get out, to try and make a go of it out there, away from all this. We've made a contact on the radio, one of the unused channels, people who can help us once we get out. The only problem is, this place was built for security. And every potential exit is crawling with them. If we can get past the outer perimeter there might be a chance."

"I think I have an idea."

"What is it?" Thorn asks.

My gaze jumps from him to Rose and back to Eva. The plan for my own escape falls into place, as well as theirs. "Can you find me a map of the compound?"

Thirteen

Three days later, we gather in the rec room.
Word had spread about the escape, but we had to be careful the wrong people didn't hear it. The others begin to arrive, nervous energy filling the room. The map of the compound spreads out before us on the ping pong table.

"There is an exit here," I point to the red jagged field on the map. "I almost didn't see it because it's on one of the basement levels below the ground floor."

"Basement One," Rose interjects. "Ash, it's filled with them. From Basement One on down. There are dozens, if not hundreds of creatures down there. We'll never get past them?"

"I will," I say.

A slow dawning reaches all of their expressions.

"What's the plan?" Rose asks.

"The easy part is going to be getting me out," I say. "I can walk right past them. Once I'm out, I'll connect with our outside contact. Eva has arranged for them to give me a vehicle or two. Then we'll come back for all of you. This is where it get's a little tricky. One of the vehicles will have to break through the wall, here." I point to the highlighted line on the map.

"The library," Rose says, her brow furrowing in concentration.

"We load everyone up, here. We'll have to move quickly. The noise and activity will attract the zombies around the perimeter, but once everyone is inside the vehicles and moving again, you'll be perfectly safe. Any questions so far?"

"Sounds simple enough," says Bertrand with a slight chuckle, placing a protective hand over his daughter's shoulder.

"Someone will need to make sure everyone is here when we return. Once I'm out, we're planning for a one day turn around. I'll be back this time tomorrow night,"

"I'll make sure," Thorn says. I had almost forgotten his presence, leaning up against the wall at the other side of the table. "I'll get everyone to the library."

I give him a quick nod. "We'll have to move fast. Everyone will need to be ready."

"Then what?" asks one of the younger children, a girl with large frightened eyes.

"We can start over," I say.

I look at the group before me, all watching me as if seeking some kind of resolution which I cannot provide.

"Listen," I begin. "I know many of you have never been out there. You are scared, and rightly so. I've seen people die more times than I care to recall. But people learn to navigate the landscape, how to survive, and you will learn too.

"We have information that over the mountains the landscape is free of the creatures. If we can get you there, all of you can live without having to worry about them."

"Isn't it risky?" Bertrand asks.

"Of course it's risky," I snap. A hush falls over the gathered few. "But is it worth staying and continuing to be complicit in the sick experiments going on here? In here the walls have kept you safe from the zombies. The same walls that have kept out have also kept you locked in."

“Do you think they will ever stop?” Thorn asks. “The way they think they can mess with people this way?” His expression is sharp, angled, eyes flashing and bearing down on me with ferocious intensity as if we are the only two people in the room.

“I don't think so,” I reply meeting his stare.

“It's wrong, Ash. And I'm not sorry to say, but I hate her for what she's done to you.”

It takes me a moment to pull my gaze away from his.

“Okay then,” I say. “That settles it. I go tonight. The rest of you get a good night's sleep. We have a big day tomorrow.”

“I'll walk with you,” Rose says. “If that's okay. I'll take you as far as the door.”

“It's dangerous.”

“I'll be careful.” Her expression is wide-eyed and eager. “I'll only come with you as far as I'm able.”

“Okay,” I reply.

Everyone's eyes are on us as we leave the room, but it is Thorn's lingering gaze which puzzles me the most. I have no idea what he gains from watching me the way he does. Rose and I leave the room and head down the hallway towards the stairs. I do my best to ignore the knot in my stomach.

“Basement One is two levels down from here,” she says.

I push away the memory of the sound, the awful unearthly sound of the zombies from the basement in the abandoned laboratory. We walk in silence, descending each step with careful movements. I stay in front just in case, wishing I still had the security of my weapons. We make it down the first flight, but dark shadows fall across our path. What lay in those shadows is impossible to know.

"Wait," I whisper holding out my hand to stop her. My mind extends out, taking in the space around us, feeling for anything, anyone who might be a threat. Nothing is there. "Okay, it's clear."

At the final level, we arrive at a gray unmarked door. I recall a mental image of the map, getting my bearings to where we are located. This door opens to a long dark tunnel leading underneath the outer wall, through the occupied space out on the other side of the chain link fence.

"You should go back," I say. "Get everyone ready for tomorrow. I'll make it through from here."

"They could be anywhere," she whispers. "Be careful."

I nod and place my hand on the door knob. We wait. A few moments later the lights go dark. Ten o' clock. The grid is down.

"Ash, wait."

I turn towards her, and to my surprise, she grabs me in an awkward hug.

"No matter what, I want you to know... I'm glad I got to meet you." With that, she turns and rushes back up the stairs.

I open the door and step through, pulling it closed behind me.

The sickly sweet smell of rotted flesh permeates the claustrophobic space. That sound, that broken, gasping breathing meets my ears, and my skin prickles in response. I walk forward, allowing my mind the levity to sense where they are in the darkness, seeing them without using my eyes. They turn towards me, attracted by the movement, but they make no further motions.

A strange empathy overtakes me, hearing them shuffle in place. The same doctors who perpetuated the horrors I witnessed had done this to them. They had once been persons with lives and families who loved them. The anger I feel about learning my origin stirs once more and extends to these beings around me, victims in this grand scheme like so many others. Like me.

I blink away the tears as I reach the door at the far side, pushing my way through. I walk steadily until certain I have cleared the area around the compound before I break into a run. Finding a tree, I climb to the highest branch which will support me, pull my knees to my chest and lean against the rough bark.

For the rest of the night, I am awake, scanning the horizon for the sunrise. Once daylight hits, I'll be able to travel more safely find my way to Eva's outside contact. I spot in the distance a speck on the horizon, moving down the stretch of highway, approaching through the field which appears familiar in a way I cannot pin point. The truck pulls to a stop, and immediately I recognize the driver, her long dark hair, shadowed eyes, and wicked smile aimed my way.

Alma.

"Get in," she calls through the lowered window.

My feet hit the ground in a full sprint, but my foot slips in the dew soaked grass, stumbling up the slope towards the vehicle. I scramble into the passenger side as fast as I can go, gasping to catch my breath while Alma shifts gears, tires squealing spinning out against the pavement.

"It's about time, Ash," she says once we gain traction. "We've been waiting for you."

Fourteen

The truck careens down the highway leaving a trail of black exhaust behind us, speeding away from the laboratory compound and all the horrors it contains therein. Alma presses the gas like someone on a mission.

"What are you doing here?" I ask.

Alma grins, clutching the wheel. She lifts one hand, shaping her fingers into a loose V. "Does this mean anything to you?" she asks.

"Yes, it does," I reply. "Are you in on it, too?"

She laughs. "Eden told me to do it. I have no idea what it means."

"It means I can trust you. Now, where are we headed?"

"Back to Eden's. Everyone is waiting for you."

"How far are we?" I glance backward, watching the looming edifice disappear as we veer around the bend in the road. My mind struggles to piece the information together. I turn back to face her. "Alma, we can't go back there. Eden is the one who turned me over to them. I heard her talking the night I left."

"No, Ash. It's not what you think."

"Then what is it?" The pine trees slip by on either side of us.

"When you ran out that night, Eden figured out that you had heard her talking. She put it together and realized how it must have sounded from your perspective."

"Who was she talking to?" I ask.

"Eva." Alma glances my way, her wrist resting on the

steering wheel.

"Eva!" I exclaim. "Is Eden the outside contact Eva mentioned?"

"Yeah," Alma laughs. "She is."

Another turn and we pull up to the familiar gate of Eden's farm. The dim morning sky glows just enough that I can spot Ezekiel pulling open the gate to allow us through. He pulls it closed behind us, and Alma scurries out to help him.

"Are we safe?" I ask after the final gate swings closed behind us.

"Yes," Alma answers. "We're safe, Ash. We made it."

Eden's living room is just as before, large, welcoming couch cushions and frilly tabletops. The household has already begun to stir. Down the hallway, I hear footsteps and sound of the water running as the denizens prepare for the coming day. Abraham and his unforgettable beard sit at the corner of the couch, ever watchful. His silent eyes watch us as Alma and I enter the room. Ezekiel slips in behind us.

"Right on time," Ezekiel mutters.

Eden appears out of the kitchen, wiping her hands on the gingham apron tied around her waist. Her eyes light up and she beckons us forward, her arms outstretched. She motions for me to come and sit, much like she had the first time I arrived. A bowl of thick stew appears, brimming with hearty broth and shreds of meat, followed by a plate of crumbly biscuits. I consume the food with an unmatched passion, realizing with slow dawning how it feels to be safe.

Safe.

Eden had not betrayed me after all. Alma had rescued me based on Eva's instructions. The whole group of them back at the compound are trusting me to return when night falls. The feeling is strange, foreign, but not entirely unpleasant. No one speaks as I eat, but everyone watches me with some caution. Ezekiel eyes me from the kitchen doorway, slouching against the frame. I do my best to ignore him, keeping my attention to the food before me.

"Ash," Eden speaks with a quiet, gentle voice. "I wanted to apologize about the misunderstanding. I should have been forthcoming with you from the beginning. It was never my intention to frighten you."

"It's done," I say. "I shouldn't have assumed. Thank you."

"Of course."

"You'll help me?" I ask. "Get them out I mean?"

"Yes. Eva has already communicated with us. It's how we knew where to send Alma to collect you."

Ezekiel takes a seat across from me, leaning forward and planting his elbows on the table. He shoots a glance towards Eden and then back to me before he speaks. "How does it work exactly?"

"Ezekiel!" Eden chides him.

"It's alright, Eden," I say. "I don't mind."

"So what is it? Some kind of mind control?" Ezekiel glares at me, waiting for my response.

I consider for a moment. "The truth is, I don't really know. It's not something that works all the time. It comes and goes. If I'm weak or haven't eaten for a long time it doesn't work. I think it only worked that day because I had been here for a few weeks, eating meals and getting regular sleep."

"How did you discover it?" This time it is Alma doing the asking as she sits down.

I consider for a moment before I respond. "I think the first time I realized what I could do, after leaving the compound, I mean, must have been when I was maybe eleven. I had found my way into a storage facility outside of a city, full of food. I'd never eaten so well. The plan was to set up camp and stay for a while, as long as I could. I gorged myself on peanut butter, canned pickles, dry cereal... I can't even tell you the stomach ache I had that day.

"So I went outside to get a lay of the area and to find a place to pee. They came at me fast. At the time, of course, I couldn't remember anything from my childhood, so I had no idea. It didn't help that my pants were tangled around my ankles. I knew I was done for. There were so many of them. I panicked, fell backward into the mud. That's when I noticed they had stopped moving. They stood around me, just kind of shifting from one foot to the other ignoring me."

Alma's eyes go wide as she takes in the information.

"After that, I taught myself how to do it. It took a lot of concentration. I learned the hard way that I can't do it all the time."

The image of Marcus flashes across my mind. Perhaps Eden realizes my brief discomfort somehow. She comes to my rescue with a terse interjection. "We have a lot of work to do to prepare for tonight. You should get some sleep now."

She is right.

As soon as the words are spoken, the heaviness of my exhaustion takes hold, compounded in part by the rich meal I just consumed. Alma leads me down the hall to the same room I occupied during my previous stay.

"Will you be okay?" she asks.

"Yeah. Eden is right, though. I think I just need a few hours of sleep."

"You're safe here, you know."

"I know. Thanks."

She closes the door. I am alone. This knowledge lets go of the knot in my muscles and I relax for the first time in a long time. I am not being watched by some hidden camera or nefarious scientists. I waste no time kicking off my shoes, peeling off my clothes and surrendering to the comfort of the quilted bed.

Sunlight streams through the window. The aroma of coffee and bacon drifts across my senses. My body is stiff and sore, and I feel as if I have just closed my eyes. I reach for the tee shirt crumpled on the floor next to the bed. After pulling on a clean pair of jeans, I shuffle to the dining room, circling through the kitchen to pour myself a cup of coffee.

Eden sits at the table with her coffee.

"Where did you get this?" I ask, gesturing to the steaming mug.

"A supply run from the east. Our contacts send what they can when we bring people over the mountains."

We sit in silence for a while with our coffee. This time of day, the others would be out in the gardens, checking the fences, or gathering water. Eden and I are alone in the house. She stands and walks over to the window.

"I know what they're doing up there," she says. "In that laboratory."

I do not answer. The knowledge hangs between us in the silence, an invisible blight that cannot be undone.

"They stay up there," she continues. "Believing they can change things, believing they can fix it. They can't. None of us can. We've done this to ourselves, you know. I don't know. Maybe they can fix it in the end, but I don't think so. This is the world we live in now."

"Did you know her? Doctor Donovan, I mean?"

She stands still, gazing out the window, the sloping landscape. Her reply is so long in coming that I begin to think she has not heard me.

"Yes, I knew her," she says at last.

The sound of the others returning through the front door interrupts our reverie. Ezekiel slams through the screen door, pausing to kick off his boots. He walks through the dining room, heavy footsteps, returning from the kitchen a moment later with his own coffee and a handful of bacon strips. He slurps one into his mouth in one bite.

"Those are for lunch," Eden scolds.

Ezekiel shrugs.

She gives him a significant glance before passing him into the kitchen, our conversation either forgotten or set aside. Ezekiel returns the glare before pointing it at me. We are alone for a moment. He sets down his mug and pulls the chair across from me with a loud scrape across the floor.

"There is something I'd like to know," he says.

"What's that?" I ask sipping my coffee with raised eyebrows.

"I think you know." He still wears the same dour expression as ever, tilting his head down to glare at me from underneath his eyebrows.

I run one finger around the rim of my coffee mug. "I'll be honest with you, Ezekiel. I have no idea what your problem is with me. Care to enlighten me?"

"I think you know," he mutters.

"Seriously! Will you quit with the passive aggressive bullshit? I don't know. Other than being just another threat in this vast world of threats, I have no idea what your problem is."

He shifts in his chair. "Okay, fine. You get a free pass this time."

"What kind of free pass?"

"I watched you stop them with your mind. I saw it happen."

I think about Marcus and suppress the urge to punch Ezekiel in the face.

"Do you have any idea what people would give...?" he says. "I mean, you can basically control them, right?"

I give a slight nod. "It's not very pleasant if that makes you feel better."

His eyebrow twitches. "Maybe a little."

"Would you do it?" I ask, keeping my gaze even with his. "If you had to, would you do it?"

"Walk through a crowd of them? Are you kidding me? If I could do that, I would run this world."

I've had enough. "You keep thinking that," I snap.

"Because for me, it's a last resort. And despite what you think, there are times when it doesn't work and I have to watch people die. Do you have any free passes for that?"

He nods slowly, wheels turning behind his eyes.

"I never asked for this," I say.

"Yeah, well neither did I," he replies barely more than a whisper. "I had to watch the world fall apart around me. I mean, if my parents hadn't built this place, we wouldn't be here. We would have died along with everyone else. Sometimes I wish we had. But I used to go to school. I had friends and everything. It was nice. I may not have thought so at the time, but it was nice.

"Then the whole world goes to hell. Everyone says you have a way to put it back together, back the way things were before. Something about your blood. Ash, you can save everyone if you wanted to, and you don't want anything to do with it. The truth is, you are nothing more than a selfish little girl."

I lean back in my seat, his words stinging. Staring down into my coffee mug as if to search for the answer, I realize that on some base level he is right. It's true, I don't want any of it, and it's also true that this is selfish.

"They don't need me," I say. "They are trying to make another one like me. They'll get it right eventually. It's just timing, that's all. They'll find the variable."

I stand to leave but pause before exiting the room. I slowly set down the coffee mug, placing each hand on the table and lean over to speak directly into his face.

"You're one to talk, you know? Sitting here wishing for things to be how they were. You have a chance to help people out of this. You are part of something that gives people hope. Yet here you are whining about the past. It's over, Ezekiel. Moving forward is the only option. Survival is all we have left. So if I'm being selfish then you are just as guilty as I am."

I grab my empty mug and vanish to the kitchen, leaving him in my wake.

The screen door claps shut once more after Alma and Travis enter the living room. Alma's hair is pulled into a tight bun, unable to hide the uncombed tangles and bits of hay. They laugh at some shared joke as they stumble into the living room, fingers entwined.

Eden returns from the garden, arms laden with plump tomatoes which she begins to wash under the tap. I hear Ezekiel leave the dining area without another word, leaving me with a sense of unease. I make a move to help with the tomatoes and catch a glimpse of Alma, draped on the couch with her head on Travis' shoulder. For a moment I envy them, and their ability to grab these small moments of joy. Regardless, I also know there is a great deal of preparation before returning to the compound tonight. My unease will have to wait until another time.

"How many should we plan for, do you think?" Eden says.

We stand by the front door of the warehouse at the farthest edge of the property close to the tree line. At the back end of the building, two cargo doors stand open, revealing the contents inside. The left part of the structure holds a line of parked vehicles, including my blue truck. The other vehicles include a small red car with a pale brown canvas top, a rusted tractor normally driven by

Abraham in the garden, and a large white van with the words *Heavenly Blessings First Church of the Redeemer* printed in scrolling red letters along the side.

"There are at least twenty of them that I know of so far."

"Ah," Eden walks down the length of the parked vehicles, pausing in front of the truck, before resuming her slow gait. She continues until she stops in front of the white van, tapping her fingers against her chin. "We'll take out the seats. The point is to get them out quickly. We'll have to fortify the front. Let's see that map there."

I pull it from the side pocket of my backpack and hand it to her. She spreads the paper out on the slanted hood of the church van, flattening out the folded image of the compound. Squinting, she runs her finger along the path up to the line in red ink, marking the weakness in the wall, the place we must breach to get back inside.

"And you are sure they'll be waiting?" Eden says.

"They'll be ready," I say, hoping that I am right.

"And if what you say about the perimeter is right then we'll have to move fast."

"Yeah," I reply. "We'll have to beat the horde circumventing the outer walls."

"It's going to be risky. If they're not there for some reason..."

"They'll be there," I say.

Eden steps back from the map. "There is one more thing, Ash."

"What is it?"

She motions for me to follow. The other side of the warehouse is divided into walled cubicles. One is filled with dry goods, toilet paper, toothpaste, and other commodities. The next shelf contains canned food items, shelves of glass jars, sealed most likely by Eden herself in preparation for the coming doomsday.

"Ah, here." Eden approaches the third alcove. "I believe we have something which belongs to you."

Among the weapons, long guns, and blades, I spot my crossbow. Alone on a shelf, fully stocked quiver with the safety latch still on. Eden steps forward lifting it with one hand under the barrel. She extends my weapon with an apologetic smile. "I think you might be needing this?"

The weight of my weapon in my hands makes me realize how much I missed having it with me, the feeling of security, and yes, the thrill of victory at watching one of those monsters crumple when my aim is true. Having it back is the closest thing to home that I know.

"Thank you," I whisper, tucking the strap over my shoulder. "Thank you, Eden."

She offers a quick smile before turning her attention back to the vehicles.

Fifteen

The two vehicles trundle along the outer edge of the compound wall, a large, looming edifice alongside the road. The white van is fortified with planks of metal welded to the front, a wedge of steel, added by Eden and some of the others earlier in the day. I sit in the back of the blue truck, which is following behind the van, my crossbow resting on my knees.

"Ready for acceleration," Travis says, his voice crackling through the walkie-talkie clipped to my belt.

Ezekiel picks up to return the message. "Ten-four, good buddy!"

I give him a nod through the window, lifting the crossbow and shifting my weight to press up against the cab for the impact. The ground gets rough as we veer off the road towards the gap in the chain link fence. My stomach flip-flops as the air rushes past me. The vehicle's noise is gaining the attention of a huddle of zombies cresting the slope of the landscape. I crouch and brace myself. Several seconds pass as we ricochet over the rough terrain, building momentum.

The wall hurtles towards us.

We hit hard.

My feet scoot out from under me on impact as we breach the wall. Both vehicles screech to a halt. We are inside the library. A gaping, jagged hole appears through the settling dust. In the distance, a gathering clutch of zombies lurches towards us, drawn by the explosion of sound.

I stand and lean against the cab, taking in the surroundings.

Someone had pushed over the shelves. There is a sea of broken books surrounding the two vehicles. In the clearing haze, I spot Thorn opening the door of the van, already escorting the others inside, as easy as clockwork. He catches my eye and we exchange a quick nod.

"Get in the middle," I call over the group. "And stay down, away from the windows!"

The first edge of the clutch filters through, a hive of errant ants. We do not have much time before the place will be filled with them. The door to the library rattles and Thorn's head whips around. I notice that one of the bookshelves leans up against the doors, locking us inside. Whatever happened, they've been pursued. I keep my arrow aimed at the door. Travis rolls down the window on the driver's side, arching out his head to check the surroundings.

"Go!" Thorn calls, sliding the door shut and slapping the side of the van.

The van's wheels spin out against the carpet as Travis struggles to turn the steering wheel. Thorn jogs over and leaps into the truck bed with me, just as our makeshift caravan pulls forward.

"Get in the cab!" I yell as Thorn hops over the tailgate. "It's safer there."

"No time," comes his reply.

"Then stay down and don't get in my way."

The creatures lurch past us, unable to grasp anything. I don't feel bad about them taking over the compound. As large as this place is, the people inside must have a safe room to hide in. They have more at their disposal than they would ever let on.

We surge forward. I shift to my knees and scoot forward to the end of the truck bed, aiming the bow out over the tailgate. Thorn is behind me, crouched and huddled. Already, I can see that more zombies are joining the herd. I cannot shoot them all. I pick up the walkie-talkie.

"We have to plow through," I say.

"We've already punched through a wall," Travis crackles. "I think we can handle a few crawlies! Let's do this!"

"Are we going to make it?" Thorn asks.

"We're going to make it," I reply.

The vehicles pick up speed. I take aim, firing off three arrows, taking down as many in the front row. They crumble to the ground, and those behind fall as their feet catch against the bodies, beginning a pile-up. I shoot again, taking down another row towards the middle. Up ahead, the van skirts the rough terrain, hopping the edge of the gravel path.

Maybe it is the mental nudge I get when they are around. I know they are there before anyone sees them. There is another horde at the edge of the tree line. If we take the road towards the farm, we'll run right into them. We are surrounded.

"What's wrong?" Thorn asks from his position against the back of the cab.

"We're not going to make it." I bring the walkie to my face. "Ezekiel, is there another path to the farm?"

"Negative," he replies. "The main drive is the only way."

"There's a wall of them coming out of the trees. Too many for me to take down."

"Can we punch through?"

I look back. We have put some distance on the compound. I have to make a decision. “I'll try my best. Just make sure you both keep the wheels on the road. Over.”

“Do your thing, Ash!” Travis interjects.

“Can you shoot?” I ask Thorn.

He nods.

“Take the bow.”

He stands and leans in, shoulder to shoulder with me. Concentrating is difficult with the movement of the vehicles, but I do my best to tune everything out. Immediately, I feel something different about them. They are communicating with each other. The ones behind us have somehow beckoned the ones coming out of the forest. The link is strong and animal, nothing but desire and hunger.

I find it, letting my mind stretch out. My breath catches. I push back.

They ease away, slowing their shuffling steps. Not enough. There are too many of them. I push back harder, the energy leaving my body. To my left, Thorn shoots an arrow at the first one appearing out of the tree line, catching it in the shoulder. I close my eyes, relax my mind, and push again.

They hit the van like a tidal wave, but somehow both vehicles stay upright. They slide around us. Using every ounce of strength left in me, I push against them once more. A bubble of space begins to form around the two vehicles, sliding in tandem down the road. I don't realize I am shaking until I feel Thorn's arms around my shoulders, guarding me as I keep them at bay. The truck plunges forward, my hair whipping in the wind.

"Yeeeeehaw!" Travis shouts from the open window up ahead, pounding the flat of his hand against the metal frame of the door. I keep my concentration focused, squeezing my eyes closed, finding the connection with them and pushing... pushing... pushing them away.

My eyes open when the vehicle comes to a stop. We are inside the first layer of fencing and Ezekiel is jogging to pull the gate closed behind us, locking us into safety. Alma has come out to meet us and is pulling open the second gate.

"Are we safe?" I gasp.

"We're safe," Thorn says, his arms still wrapped around my shoulders. "We're safe, Ash. We made it."

Travis and Alma lead the new arrivals into the house, offering assurances. Thorn stays with me, both of us collapsed against each other in the back of the truck bed. We wait until everyone is inside before we move.

Eden's living room is filled with people. She is in her element, handing out fresh warm rolls and cups of hot coffee. Against the back of the room, Travis lounges on the couch, absently rubbing his left arm. Alma sits draped next to him, eyeing the new arrivals. Bertram comforts Iris, offering her a sip of his coffee. Across from them, the twins sit wide-eyed with their parents on either side. These new arrivals have never been outside the safety of the compound. The collective relief is palpable.

But something feels off.

I scan the room watching for anything amiss. Chatting, coaxed smiles from the gathered few, Alma leaning in and laughing at something Travis just said, his hand resting lightly on her thigh. I wander back to the door, stepping out into the night air.

Moments later, Travis steps out next to me. Without a word he extends his arm out, pulling back the flannel sleeve. In the glow of the moonlight, the clear crescent-shaped outline of a bite mark stands out against his pale flesh.

"Travis--" I gasp.

"Guess I should have rolled up the window, huh?" he says.

The flickering embers float into the darkening evening sky from the funeral pyre at the top of the mountain. Three days have passed since the rescue from the laboratories. Everyone is gathered for Travis' funeral, knowing he is now free from the horror that may one day befall each one of us. Abraham and Eden each give a eulogy befitting of one who had been a vital part of their community. Alma stands next to me, pinched and silent. She had stayed with him right up to the end, holding his hand and mopping his fevered forehead until it was no longer safe to do so.

The following week consists of everyone preparing for the coming journey. I am assigned to teach knife skills to those ready and able to learn. We gather in the fields outside the warehouses. Now that I know which direction to look, I can just make out the distant outline of the laboratories on the horizon, a blemish in an already broken world. We all meet up after lunchtime for a series of drills, everyone lined in rows, waiting for my instructions.

"I need everyone to partner up today," I say.

They shuffle around and adjust position. They know from previous sessions to pair up one adult and one child so they can each take turns practicing. I notice Thorn is the odd one out, so I motion him over to partner with me.

"Don't worry," I say. "I'll go easy on you."

He pulls up one corner of his mouth and takes position across from me.

"Imagine," I begin facing the gathered few. "One of you is the approaching creature. Take turns doing this. The fastest way to take one down coming straight on is to sidestep and jab them in the ear. They move slowly, so most of the time this technique is not that difficult. Go ahead and try it."

Half of them start the pantomime, stumbling towards their partners. There are some giggles from the younger ones. I motion for Thorn to approach me. He rolls his eyes back and hangs his mouth slack in his affected performance. I lunge and mime stabbing him in the ear, and he collapses to the ground, twitching and hacking until his dramatic end. I give him an extended slow clap and everyone joins in the applause, laughing at his exaggerated performance.

I reach out my hand to help him to his feet.

"If you don't have a weapon," I continue, gathering everyone's focus. "It is possible to sever the spinal cord by hand. It's not optimal, but it's good to know how in case you find yourself in that situation. I'll show you first and then you try it."

I mime the action, placing my hands on the side of Thorn's head, checking my motions as I pantomime twisting his head around. He play-acts, collapsing while lunging forward. Our feet tangle, sending us both into a fallen heap on the ground in an awkward pile. I land on top of him, face to face. Blood rushes to my cheeks.

We both leap to our feet, brushing off our clothes.

"If that should happen out there," I say to the watching class. "You are pretty much done for, so watch your footing."

"What else can you tell us about them?" Iris asks.

Everyone turns towards me, waiting for my answer. I realize in that moment that most, if not all of them, have never experienced life outside of the laboratory compound. They've never come face to face with a zombie out in the wild, as I have. They are looking to me to prepare them for that. I only hope I am up to that task.

"They move slowly," I reply. "Unless instigated. They respond to noise more than anything else. They can't climb or figure out problems, so if you need to get away fast, climbing a tree or finding a high level is a good short-term solution."

"How many of them are out there?" Bertram asks, placing his hand protectively over Iris's shoulder.

"Less than there used to be. They are most dangerous in groups. Don't think you can outrun them, either. You can go as fast and as far as you can, but eventually, you'll get tired. They never will."

Eden approaches at the edge of the field, hanging back and watching.

"What's most important," I say. "Is this. If you can get away, do it. Don't take them on unless you absolutely have to. Does everyone understand that?"

Everyone nods, slow and solemn.

"We have a hard journey ahead. My goal is for everyone to

make it."

"Excellent work, Ash," Eden says taking a step forward. "You have done a wonderful thing by sharing your knowledge with us. These lessons have served us all well."

She turns her attention to the group.

"I have just received word that the caravan will be arriving at dawn. We need to be completely ready by sunset. And I want all of you to get plenty of rest. Ash is right. You all have a hard journey ahead."

Her eagle-eyes survey the group. She offers a quick smile and with a flick of the wrist dismisses everyone. They filter back one by one. Eden catches my eye, giving me a knowing look before following the others back to the house.

I pick up my crossbow, the weight of the strap on my shoulder feeling like an old friend.

Thorn leans against the tree with his arms crossed, watching me from under his eyebrows. I pause and wait for him, wary, crossing my arms and matching his gaze. He stares me down with a bizarre intensity that unnerves me.

"I wanted to talk to you before we leave tomorrow," he says.

"About what?"

"Look." He takes a step towards me. "This isn't easy for me to say, but I know anything could happen. Ash, listen to me for a second, okay?"

"I'm listening."

"I've never met anyone like you before."

"Thanks for the reminder, Thorn," I mutter.

"No, I don't mean it that way." He rubs his palm over the back of his hair, staring out towards the horizon. "I'm talking about..."

"What *are* you talking about?" I say, an eruption of annoyance rising up inside me.

"I like you, Ash," he says, matter of fact. "I can't go out there without telling you that. That's all. You don't have to say anything back, but I wanted you to hear it."

I don't answer, but stand there unmoving, arms still crossed.

He tucks one hand into his back pocket, the other hanging limp at his side. His gaze is steady, not wavering from mine. Blood rushes to my cheeks and I can't tell if it is anger, annoyance or something else. He makes a move to head back towards the cabin.

"Hang on!" I snap before he gets too far. "Come back."

"What?" His voice carries a tinge of hope.

"How dare you say that to me, Thorn."

His mouth opens as if to speak, but he hesitates, eyes dilating.

I continue, making no effort to hide my ire. "You have no idea what's out there. I've lived out there, and you have no *clue* what it takes to survive. Do you honestly think that telling me about your little crush is some kind of heroic gesture? This world has no place for that, Thorn. None."

He shuffles his feet but keeps his gaze steady on me.

"You want to know what I've been doing all this time?" I say. "Watching people die, Thorn."

He steps back, his jaw opening slightly. A muscle in his cheek twitches under his skin.

“I've seen more people die than you have met in your life probably. Think about that. I mean, this last mission was planned to the minute and look what happened to Travis.”

“Travis was stupid. He should have been more careful.”

“Yes, exactly. In this world, that is how people die. I don't know why he left the window down, but he did. And now he's gone. Every second out there counts. If you look the wrong way, you could die. If you take the wrong turn, you could die. If you don't hear them coming, you could die. My constant focus is on staying alive for the next five minutes and keeping everyone around me alive too. There is no room for anything else. Do you comprehend that at all?”

He nods.

“Good. Now if you don't mind, I need to go and fill my water canteen.” I keep my eyes on him until he turns to walk back to the cabin. At least he is not there to see my hands tremble as I unhook the canteen from my belt.

“The drivers are ready.” Abraham steps out the front door, heading off to the row of vans parked just inside the fence. Everyone is up, having eaten a large breakfast, perhaps our last for a while, and now filter back and forth from their bedrooms to the living room.

Pausing in the entryway, I double check my crossbow, arrows, and knives, lightly touching the holster at my ankle. Two more drivers had arrived from another location to the West, more contacts within the web to get people over the mountain to safety. I see them preparing supplies in the back hatches of the caravan.

Eden taps my elbow as the last of them step out the door. "I wanted to catch you before you leave," she says.

"You aren't... you're not coming with us?"

"No," she says. "My place is here." She places a plump hand over her heart.

"Oh," I glance out to the gathered, scattered casually around the caravan. "I didn't realize, but I guess you are right."

"In the meantime, Ash, I want to go over the defensive strategies."

"Of course, yes."

"The front and back vehicles will have defense. You'll be in the middle van. I want you to keep your weapons at the ready. The path over the mountain is clear according to our last communication, but there are some spots which may be thick with zombies."

"I understand," I say, nodding at her words.

"I know we have the look-outs, and everyone has been briefed on what to expect, but do you think you could.... you know."

"I'll look out for them," I reply understanding her implication.

She smiles, a thin press of lips, and grabs me by the shoulders in a steely embrace. "I'll miss you, Ash," she says.

"Thank you, Eden, for everything." I allow another moment of her embrace, not knowing when, if ever, I may see her again. When she lets go, I avoid her eyes and duck out the door.

It feels strange and crowded, but I am given a seat in the front of the van. Looking around, I can see the fright of the unknown is replaced with the oncoming excitement of the journey. I spot Eva at the edge of the group, crouched down to get eye level with Iris, flanked on each side by Sam and Eliot. Eva catches my gaze and offers a quick wave.

I smile and wave back.

The driver sitting next to me is Simeon, a dark-skinned man with a thick Jamaican accent. We had chatted briefly over breakfast when he told me he does these runs in exchange for supplies which he takes back to his family just east of the Mississippi. He offers me a grin, reaching up to open a crack in the sunroof.

The wheels emit a low hum as the vehicle slips off the gravel road and onto the pavement. The caravan pulls out, a train of three. Through the back window, I catch a glimpse of Abraham standing at the door with his arms crossed. Eden stands next to him, a serene smile drifting across her expression. We turn the bend and they are out of sight.

Sixteen

We drive for hours, filling the time with lost songs and made-up games. Now with evening approaching, everyone sits quietly, either snoozing or staring at the passing countryside. Up ahead, the black jags of the mountain range juts into the pin pricked starlight, bright Venus hanging low on the horizon. The square of light in the rear view mirror glows a deep orange, reflecting the setting sun. Simeon hums an unfamiliar tune under his breath, murmuring lyrics about country roads and West Virginia.

"What is this place up ahead?" I ask.

"That, my dear, was once called the Blue Ridge Mountains. They are beautiful."

"They are," I say. Even in the darkness, I can tell he is right.

We make a pit stop at a place in the valley where we can see in all directions but one, a deep forest running alongside the edge of the road. The caravan rolls to a stop, engines idling in a low hum. I stand alert at the door, one foot propped on the door handle and the other perched on the hood, giving me only a slight advantage to the landscape.

Up at the front van, a young man with an arm length arrow tucked over his shoulder climbs up to stand on the roof. Everyone pairs up, taking turns around the edge of the hill to do their business. I grab my backpack and hand out snacks, oat clusters and beef jerky to those gathered. Talk is minimal. We don't want to attract any unwanted guests.

Iris returns first, the twin's mother following behind her, keeping watch over the children. The young girl's eyes are wide, staring past the caravan. She points a trembling finger towards the tree line. The lookout up ahead lets out a low whistle, signaling danger. The sound prompts everyone to scurry for the shelter of the vans.

They appear out of the forest's edge, stumbling and lurching just out of the treeline. There is no way to know if there are more behind them. The lookout in the front van tucks his way inside, standing with his head and shoulders sticking out of the sunroof. Three of them and only four arrows left in his quill.

Unlike me, he uses an old-fashioned bow and arrow. He knows what he is doing too, based on his stance. He narrows his eyes, placing an arrow. The zombies are still some distance away. That is going to be one hell of a shot. I hold my breath, watching. Three. Two. One.

Down goes the one closest to him, the still trembling arrow sticking out of his forehead, gaping mouth turned towards the stars. He pulls another arrow. Down goes the second. I focus on the edge of the forest, watching for more. He can handle these three. Of this, I have no doubt. Even so...

"I have a bad feeling, Simeon," I murmur.

The third one falls into a motionless heap.

We are clear.

He climbs back into the safety of the van, idling the engine and nudging forward. Simeon reaches up and closes the sunroof above us.

"Just in case," he says with an assuring grin.

That's when the rest of them emerge from the trees, many more than I can count. The zombies appear out of the shadows as if made of the gloom darkening the trees. So many, it quickly becomes impossible to distinguish them from the tree trunks. They pile into the grassy moonlit area between the tree line and the road's shoulder.

"Shit," I whisper, struggling to pull my crossbow from beneath my feet.

"Leave it. There's no room for that." Simeon reaches for the walkie-talkie.

"Driver One, come in," he barks.

"I see them," comes the crackling reply.

"We need to clear this. Everyone hit the gas and stay in formation. Driver Three, stay on my tail. You copy?"

I hold on to the edge of the dashboard, calculating the distance it will take for us to clear the edge of the horde before they reach the road. "It's going to be close," I say soft enough that only Simeon can hear me.

He nods and lifts the speaker to his lips. "This is Driver Two. All drivers copy?"

"Ten-four!" Driver One squawks.

"Ten-four!" Driver Three calls, a tinge of panic in her voice.

"Ten-four." Simeon echoes before handing the device over to me.

I hold it loose, keeping it available for him if he needs it in a moments notice. I glance back to check on the others. They all have their faces pressed towards the window, watching helplessly as we move with agonizing speed. The only way out is to race against the pace of the shuffling monsters creeping towards us.

"Come on," Simeon murmurs, eyes darting between the road ahead and the rear view mirror.

In the middle row, Eliot begins to cry, a small and helpless sound. Simeon and I both know we can't afford to frighten the passengers any more than they already are. I turn back to Eliot in an attempt to offer some comfort, to get him quiet. We can't afford any sound with those things this close to us. All we need is to get past this line and then we will be in the clear.

Placing my fingers to my lips, I shake my head, hoping he understands. Eliot's mother wraps her arms around him to calm his tears, trying to mask the small snuffling sound emitting from him. He buries his face in her arms and quiets while she strokes his back.

They are now about ten yards from the edge of the road. I place my palms flat against the dashboard willing myself calm with the realization that everything is out of my hands. There are too many of them out there. I have no way to shoot them. Weapon defense is pointless right now anyway. There are too many of them to take down and munitions would only draw their attention towards us. We surge forward, staying as close to the other vehicles as possible.

Simeon grabs the speaker from my hand and snaps a command into it. "It's getting close back there! We need some room!"

"Copy that," The driver behind us replies.

The distance grows between the vans. Simeon presses on

the gas, knocking me back in my seat. I turn just in time to catch a glimpse of the herd clipping into the side of the van behind us. The driver's face curls into a snarl as she attempts to swerve, mowing down the three which had stumbled in front of her. The rest of them pile up, slowing the vehicle, gunking up the tires. I hear the whine of the engine struggling against the added friction.

"Come on," I whisper. "You can make it."

Simeon glances through the rear view. "There is nothing we can do. We have to move on."

I turn back to the front before I hear the huge explosion. At first, I think a spark had caught the gas line taking out the back vehicle, but a quick glance to the mirror shows the van bursting through the creatures, sending them flying in all directions. I resist the urge to cry out in joy. The caravan surges forward, escaping the clutches of danger.

We made it. All of us.

It takes some time for everyone to calm down after the near miss, but at last the adrenaline wears off and everyone falls asleep. Simeon continues driving, even though I offer to take over.

"It's my job," he says. "You just keep watch."

I settle back in my seat, watching the passing lines in the road.

"Once we reach the tree line, we'll be safer," he says. "Apparently they can't climb."

"I wonder why not," I say. "I mean I know they can't take the stairs, but what stops them from following the switchbacks? The roads are clear enough, right?"

"Some of them try to," he says, "but they don't think to follow the road. They aren't very bright you know. It's not much different from how they pile up at the bottom of a staircase."

"I see." I turn to watch him, the lights of the dashboard gleaming blue against his wizened face. "What did you do? I mean, before. You know."

"I was an accountant, believe it or not."

"An accountant?" I give a small chuckle trying to imagine this hardened man sitting behind a desk. "I've read about that. You don't seem the type."

He echoes my amusement. "I'm good at adjusting to changing circumstances."

"Aren't we all," I say.

We continue onward, our fare sleeping soundly in the back. The roads are even as we make our way up the first mountain, slowing at each hairpin curve. I imagine what lies ahead, daring to glimpse the fleeting feeling of safety dancing just at the edge of possibility.

"What is that, up ahead," Simeon says. He lifts the speaker of the walkie to his lips. "Driver One, this is Driver Two. What's the situation up there?"

"Bridge out." The crackled voice comes back. "We're going to have to hike across. Leave the vehicles."

"Shit," he mumbles as he hands me back the walkie.

The caravan slows to a stop and I jump out, leaving the others to sleep. The drivers gather to consider the options while the guard takes his place on top of the van to keep watch.

"The rains must have washed it out," Driver One says. She

is a stout woman with salt and pepper hair. No nonsense. "The water came down from the swollen crick. We'll have to camp out here. Let the kids sleep till dawn. Hike them out over the mountains."

"Can they handle it?" I ask.

"They'll have to. We can carry the little ones if we need to."

"I guess you're right. Let's circle the wagons before we lose any more light."

Before too much longer, we all crouch around the beginnings of a small fire in the middle of the road. We position the vans in a huge triangle around us, lookouts positioned at each gap. The children huddle together by the flames, sharing whispered secrets and laughter. I take my place in the assigned rotation for first watch. Climbing up the hood of the van, I pull a slab of jerky from my backpack, gnawing at the meat while gazing off into the darkness of the surrounding forest. I know we are safe from the creatures, but who knows what else might be hiding in the darkness.

"Hey there," Thorn walks up with something in his hand. He climbs up the hood and sits down next to me, handing me a sandwich.

"Thanks," I say.

He peers into the forest next to me. Despite myself, it feels nice, having him here, sitting silently. I don't want to talk, but I don't like the feeling hanging over us, the sense of the unsaid.

"Hey, um..."

"Yeah?" he replies a bit too quick.

"I just wanted to say... I didn't mean to... I mean..." My

mind spins as I try to pinpoint the right words.

"It's okay, Ash," he says with a crooked grin. "You don't have to say anything about, you know. About before."

"Okay, good," I breathe. "Because I really didn't want to."

He chuckles just a bit, and I smile.

"Do you think it will be okay to hike them out, like she said?" I ask glancing down at the sleeping children tucked in their bags.

"They'll be fine." He rubs his hand across the back of his neck, ruffing up the edge of hair along his collar. We sit for a while, side by side, with no words or expectations. A sudden yawn overtakes me, deep and shuddering. I turn away from him covering my mouth with the back of my hand until I catch my breath.

"Hey, there's an empty seat over in the van," he says. "If you want to take a nap. I'll keep an eye on the kids."

Fatigue washes over me. Sleep doesn't sound too bad. "Okay, just for a little while," I say.

Thorn slides off the van and holds my hand, supporting me as I climb down the hood again. For half a second we stand face to face in the moonlight, close enough that I feel his breath on my cheek. I step back, my fingers slipping away from his grasp.

I make my way to the van and stretch out in the passenger seat, leaving the door open to the night air. I stretch and arch my back against the reclined seat, working out the kinks before leaning back, taking a breath and closing my eyes.

Morning arrives with a slow dawning of light behind my closed eyes. I wake to the sensation of cold damp clinging to my exposed skin. Already, the parcel of children have escaped into the forest to take care of their morning needs at the designated tree just outside of camp. Everyone wakes, some gathering around the fire to warm their hands before we make the effort to cross the river.

We line up, Thorn on one end, Alma, Rose, and then myself at the far side. The water swirls around our bare feet, icy but bearable. I plant my feet into the muddy riverbed, waiting as the children make their way across first. They send Iris over. She carefully clings to one person at a time as we pass her hand over hand, her feet inches from the fast moving water. She lands safe on the other side of the river, slipping out of my grasp.

With obvious relief, she scurries over to the large oak tree to wait for the rest of us. Once the children are over, everyone else picks their way across, hopping from stone to stone or balancing on the fallen logs. Gathered at the other side, Alma passes out slivers of jerky.

"We need to keep our energy up," she says. "There's still quite a way to go."

We begin the forward march, following the switchbacks. I pull my backpack around my shoulders, pinning my crossbow snugly to my back. Everyone moves in silence, traveling along the pavement. The children walk in the middle, carrying the backpacks each had been given, while the rest of us form a circle around them in formation. If not for the impending threat of certain death, the sun-dappled path would be pleasant.

The sound of a shrill whistle cuts through the forest, a warning from the point guard up ahead.

I drop my pack and swing the crossbow around into a

defensive position.

Everyone stands still. The signal sounds again, echoing through the mountainside, bouncing off the rocks. I glance at Alma.

She shrugs.

I don't sense the approach of any zombies, but I press my finger alongside the bow's cold metal trigger. I scan the tree line, waiting for something, anything to happen. The sound of shuffling feet, the lurching crunch of branches and leaves, anything unnatural. I whirl my crossbow, focusing the scope to a whisper of motion at the road's shoulder.

A small brown rabbit hops across the leaf-strewn path.

They step out of the forest, surrounding us on all sides, fifty of them at least, all armed, weapons at the ready. Humans, nothing more. A motley group, but even the old ones carry a steely gaze, hardened and worn. They wear clothing that may have fit them at some point in time but now hang off their skeletal, hungry bodies.

A woman steps forward, dressed far nicer than the rest of them. Black leather boots tied up her legs, stopping just under the knee. Her crisp, blue-jeans fit snug against her slender frame. Her skin is perhaps most noticeable, healthy and pink, a look unique to those who have a constant supply of food. Around her head, she wears a white bandanna wrapped around long brown hair. Her arm drapes around our point guard's shoulders, the blade glinting sunlight against his neck.

"Good afternoon, y'all," she says in a thick southern drawl. "I'm assumin' this here's one a yours?"

No one moves.

This is a raiding party.

I scan the group, trying not to draw attention to myself. They outnumber us, there's no doubt about that, but we may still have the advantage. All of their eyes are cast towards her, perhaps waiting for a signal. I do not miss this detail. Their attention is diverted to her. I take note.

Behind the woman is a cluster of children, scabby, thin, and desperate. One brown mop of hair stands out above the others. A lanky boy, wide-eyed, and in need of a good meal. I recognize him on sight.

Marcus.

Marcus!

My breath catches in my throat and I will him not to notice me. He does, his eyes meeting mine and growing even wider. I shake my head only enough for him to see.

Don't, I plead silently. *Don't, Marcus.*

He stays where he is, but watches me with a wild ferociousness.

"Well," the woman continues, drawing my attention back to her. "Y'all are about as quiet as a Quaker meetin'. Either he's yours or he ain't. Perhaps I'm mistaken and I can do us both a favor and dispatch him? We wouldn't want him givin' away our position, right?"

"He's one of ours," I say stepping forward. I keep my bow level on her. "And you are going to let him go, so we can be on our way."

She glances me over, taking in every inch of my frame. Her laughter sounds like flint rock. "Well now, bless your heart! Why would I do such a thing when you have so many pretty toys?" Her eyes linger over the children sheltered behind us.

"Because if you take so much as one step towards us, I am going to put this arrow through your skull. You may kill him before you die, but we will have lost only one. Your people will scatter, get picked off one by one. You already know there is a horde coming up the mountain behind us. It's only a matter of time before they get here."

Her smile stays frozen in place, but her eyes widen.

"You know I'm right," I say. "None of us would survive."

"Is that so? And who are you to make such a threat?" Her voice is silky smooth as if the surrounding circumstances are an everyday occurrence. Perhaps for her, they are.

"My name is Ash, and you should know, if I pull this trigger, I won't miss."

"I believe you, darlin'," she drawls. "And yes, I've heard about you. You're the one keeping them at bay, aren't you."

It is not a question.

"At ease, fellas," the woman says. "There's nothing good here anyway."

She drops the knife and steps back, palms up in a gesture of surrender. The point guard runs forward until he is behind the safety of our defensive line. He rubs his neck and turns back, pulling his own knife from his ankle sheath and joining us in formation. I allow my gaze to flick towards Marcus once more. He trembles, watching me with palpable desperation.

"That boy," I say as my heart races. "That one there. He comes with us."

The woman's expression shifts to one of mild amusement. "Oh?"

"A gesture of good will," I continue. "A peace offering."

She places her knife in its sheath at her waist and rubs her hands against her jeans. I still have the crossbow trained on her forehead. Glancing at the children behind her, she once again cuts her eyes back to us, crossing her arms over her chest. "Fine," she mutters, signaling him towards us with a toss of her head.

Marcus runs towards us, tucking himself into the center with the other children. The surrounding raiders step back into the forest. I keep my bow at the ready and we all hold our stance until the sound of their footsteps fade away in the distance.

My crossbow clatters against the pavement as I take a knee, but Marcus' steely arms around my neck and shoulders still throw me off balance. "How are you alive?" I ask struggling to form words around the tears. "How? I saw them take you? Oh, Marcus! I'm so sorry! I'm so, so sorry."

He weeps into my shoulder, clinging to me as much as I to him. He is thinner than when I lost him, but the same fire still flickers behind his eyes. We stay that way for I don't know how long, until gentle hands, Alma's, touch my shoulders. I pull back, swipe my palms across my cheeks, drying away the sticky tears. It takes several minutes before I can steady my breath.

"We need to go," Alma says softly.

"I know," I reply. "I wasn't bluffing about that horde."

We stand and walk onward in silence, keeping the formation of the group. Everyone besides me keeps their weapons at the ready, knowing we will not be safe until we reach the checkpoint. Marcus clings to my hand, not wavering from my side. He does not speak but watches me with big wondering eyes.

"You're like me aren't you," I say. "That's why you are still alive?"

He nods.

"Did you know?" I ask.

He nods again.

"That's what you were trying to tell me that night, wasn't it? I guess on some level I already knew."

He smiles, just a hint of movement at the corner of his lips.

"I'm sorry about your mother."

He shakes his head.

"But I guess she wasn't your mother, was she?"

He shakes his head again, a flicker of sadness in his eyes, offset by the motion of his hand swinging my arm back and forth. Rose and Alma walk ahead of us, side by side, helping each other up the slopes and rocky segments of the overgrown path. Thorn walks with some of the others, a few steps behind us.

"There they are!" Simeon exclaims in a stage whisper loud enough for all of us to hear. One by one, our steps speed up, as the group realizes the end of the long journey has arrived. In the distance, headlights cut through the darkening trees, snaking down the opposite mountainside and illuminating the pavement. The last of the setting sun gleams off the windshield of the distant vehicle, piercing my vision.

"It's the rendezvous," Simeon says. "There they are!"

"Who are they?" I ask. "What does it mean?"

"It means, Ash," Alma says with a grin. "That we're going

home."

Simeon waves his hands over his head, signaling our position. Through the break in the trees, we step out onto a paved overlook. Alma and Rose stand hand in hand. Thorn steps ahead, taking in the view. The relief is palpable in all of us, standing speechless, some taking swigs of water from canteens and plastic bottles.

Mountaintops roll towards the distance, an ocean of pine-colored waves. With my free hand, I reach forward and slip my fingers into Thorn's hand. He starts with surprise, glancing at me, but I keep my gaze forward. His muscles relax, and he closes his hand around mine. The five of us stand amid the group, side by side in the fading light. Alma's words echo in the whisper of wind with the possibility of a new life awaiting us over the ridge.

She is right.

We are going home.

End

About the Author

R.G. Westerman has been writing nearly her whole life and has a number of short stories available on Amazon through various anthologies. She loves to explore and create stories about problems she will never have, such as oncoming zombie hordes and other creatures of the fantastic!

When not creating tales of horror and whimsy, R.G. can be found hiking the mountain trails of Appalachia. She occasionally dabbles in freelance and endures her fabulous day job. She currently lives in the mountains of East Tennessee with her husband and two genius children. Rising Ash is her first published novel.

Made in the USA
Middletown, DE
15 October 2017